MW01277850

The Corner

Laura Rissmiller-Dennis

Copyright © 2018 Laura Rissmiller-Dennis

All rights reserved.

ISBN-13:
978-1983595547

ISBN-10:
1983595543

DEDICATION

As Ernest Hemingway once wrote, "There's nothing to writing. All you do is sit down at a typewriter and bleed." I never fully understood this until I realized that any writing is a true giving of yourself – your blood – the inner essence of you. That is what this book is, truly. Having ideas stuck in my head for years and years, a story in the barest of form. The inkling of ideas that had to be put to writing before they drove me mad. This story wanted to break free and to become something living.

I realize, now, that this is the true gift, and curse, of a writer. The smallest glimpses of what *could* be swimming around in my brain, but no idea of how to chisel them into something readable. One day, I sat down at my computer and it just poured out – all my blood. Line after line coming to life. The bare bones of these ideas, these memories, were forming into something palpable. Yet, I doubted myself, so I stopped writing. Until my best friend, my then husband, Jason, asked me if my book was finished.

My book. Those words resonated with me. I had written a *book* hadn't I? It was there, mostly, just needed to be concluded. What was I afraid of? I had been writing my entire life, why was this different? This was personal, a labor of love, a dedication to my childhood, an ode to my memories. I was afraid to send it out into the world for fear of being rejected, or worse, told I couldn't write! I didn't want my life to be a farce. Being a writer was part of my identity.

I realized so many people had shown faith in my ability to write. From my earliest days my parents were eager to read anything I produced, always being supportive and lovingly critical. My Mom instilled in me a love of reading, which fostered my love of writing. She helped me to enter young authors contests in grade school – my very first rudimentary books. Others along the way, from teachers to professors, have told me that I had talent, a voice.

This is for you. For all of you who have read my stories, my plays, my poems and who have encouraged me. This is for my children, Cameron and Griffin, may you never give up on your dreams and know that if you want it badly enough, you can do it. Don't let fear be a dictator in your life – dream it and do it. Most importantly, this is for Jason, my very best friend, who allowed me the time and space to create this, always having faith in me.

Finally, it is for all of you who know this corner, and who hold its memory fondly in your hearts as well. You know who you are.

ACKNOWLEDGMENTS

This book truly couldn't have come to fruition without so many people. My Mom and Dad who really did endure my rambunctious, and quite frankly, ridiculous behavior. My teachers along the way who encouraged me to write, and who realized that writing was a very important outlet for me. My first college composition professor who told me to "Give up law, become a writer!" Jason, who listened to each revision of each paragraph each and every time without complaint – mostly. All my students and friends who I have forced this book upon, telling them to give me their honest opinions -which they did. My children, Cameron and Griffin, for whom I do everything. Finally, all my childhood friends who ran amuck with me in our small, suburban neighborhood, because that truly shaped me as a person and is the backbone of this book.

This book is definitely a labor of love and I am grateful for each and every person who has had any influence in its creation.

"Fear is pain arising from the anticipation of evil"
-Aristotle

Chapter 1

Here I stand. In *this* place.   My mind racing, my chest feeling like my heart is going to jump right out and explode. I feel like I am having an out of body experience, floating above myself.

I have no breath.

Why am I here?

It has been well over 20 years since I have stood on this cracked sidewalk square in front of this house.

My house.

The cookie-cutter houses of my once vibrant south suburban sub-division seem deserted, lonely and sad. As if the events that happened here have overtaken even the inanimate souls of these homes and caused an irreversible desolation.   The houses of this newly built subdivision, previously full of hope and promise, are now filled with a chasm of nothingness. The people who live here now have no respect for their homes, their lawns or, apparently, their neighbors. It is as if the neighborhood itself has a memory. Judgment has been passed and these homes no longer deserve respect, light, happiness or love.

Bondo-ridden, broken down cars line the curbs in perfect complement to the broken windows, unkempt lawns, graffiti adorned brick walls, barred doors and peeling paint that decorates the homes in a silent salute to who must live inside.   These houses are old and vandalized – a virtual dilapidated gingerbread lane. Not one indication of what this block used to be. No - this block is black and dark and evil. And that is fitting.

My memories of this place – my childhood home – are very strong. If I try, I can push the hard images out of my mind and recall being a child running amuck here – laughing and screaming with carefree, innocent, abandon.   As I look down the street, I imagine when these houses were new – full of hope, new families and new friends. Best friends. I can envision the houses as they once were and who had lived in each and every one – and to see what they have become saddens me in a way I can barely understand or describe.

As I stand here in the center of the block, in front of my house, I can hear music. Church music. Baptist revival church music. Full of 'ALLELUJAHS' and

'PRAIIISSSE JE-SUS.' Next to my old home is a Baptist church. I always hated living next to a church. I mean, *really* hated it. Who lives next to a church and likes it? Every Wednesday, Saturday and Sunday horrible organ music filtered out from behind the story-of-creation stained glass windows. The organic tones of "Old Rugged Cross" or "Amazing Grace" thundered loudly from that little church right into my house – into my room – and into my mind. A sort of call to pause for religion.

Praise JESUS!

   I would stand on my Holly Hobby toy box and watch the parishioners flowing in and out – wearing their Sunday bests. Dresses and heels, hats and veils, suits and ties – they always looked like they were going to a funeral. I used to wonder, "Who died? Why are they all dressed up?" Our family's religion was more lax on the dress code. Shorts or jeans were perfectly acceptable – at least you were showing up and does God really care if you are wearing tiny, white gloves?   My neighboring parishioners made it an all-day affair. I mean an ALL-DAY affair. They would gather on the steps of their worship house, talking loudly without any regard to the children who may be sleeping next door. Without any regard for *me*! They called themselves godly people, but having no regard for their neighbors is not very godly in my opinion. In fact, isn't "honor thy neighbor" a commandment? Yes, I hated living next to that church.

There was, however, one pastor whom I remember fondly. His name was Pastor Rider and he was a very cheerful man. Plump and sweaty. He had those sweat rings under his arms that seemed a permanent mark of his work for God – or at least his work on the church lawn. He carried a white handkerchief in his pocket and dabbed his brow constantly to no avail. He had what my Mom termed 'toilet seat baldness.' He was always singing and humming and went about his work with a joyful heart and a clean soul. He was very friendly and always had candy in his pocket which he shared with any of the neighborhood kids who happened to be skateboarding, biking or skating in the church parking lot when he came to work. This is not why I liked him, however. No, I liked him because of his *name*.

You see, that church had a sign out front – encased in brick – which housed an announcement board. This board listed the church name – *First Baptist Church*; the service times – *Wednesday 6:00 pm, Saturday 6:00 pm and Sunday – 8:00 am and 10:00 am*; and the best part – the Pastor's name - *J.B. Rider.* This name provided ample opportunity for the jokester children of the block, led by yours truly, to shimmy the door open and

change his name. In one, fell-swoop J.B. Rider became
B.J. Rider. This was source of much laugher from me
and my friends, and we had no idea what a "BJ" was – it
was childhood innocence at its best. We never tired of
changing that poor, sweaty man's name around and
seeing how long it took for someone to notice. Total
hilarity for us - a consistent nuisance for him. We were
bad children. More precisely, we were *badly behaved*
children. If I had known how important Pastor Rider
would eventually become to our neighborhood, and to
me, perhaps I would have given him a tad more
respect.

One of my partners in crime was my best friend Mia.
She lived six houses to the left of my house, and luckily
for her, that much further from the church. She was
an awesome friend. The kind of friend who would
pinky swear and actually mean it. The kind of friend
who you never tired of playing or having sleepovers
with. She and I hit it off the first day we met. I will
never forget it – or her. I was playing baseball with my
cousin Matt and Mia ran right up and asked to play. She
was a very pretty girl with long, curly, dirty-blonde hair.
She had stunning green eyes and an attitude to match
my own. She was as rambunctious as I was and into all
the sporty things that I liked to do. Back in 1980 not
many girls wanted to play baseball, basketball or
hockey – those things were for boys. Not me and Mia

though, we were tomboys to the hilt! I loved her right away. She could hit a line drive like nobody's business. Together we were like gum and the bottom of a shoe – you couldn't pry us apart. I never would have made it through pubescence without my Mia.

Across the street from her house was my cousin Matt's house. For the life of me I couldn't figure out why my Aunt and Uncle chose *that* house. It was putrid yellow brick with brown accents - I termed it the Wizard of Oz house. Matt was 2 years younger than I, but we got along pretty well. He had bright red hair and tons of freckles. During the summer you could barely see his skin through the mazework of freckles. He was a total trouble maker, which made him super fun. We sort of thought we had a built-in pass to be badly behaved together, because we were cousins. We assumed, incorrectly of course, that our parents wouldn't be as angry somehow if we did something we shouldn't because we were *family*. We quickly found out that it was almost exactly the opposite. I was to be a 'good example' and he was to 'know better' that I was leading him down the prim rose path of despicable behavior. I think we led each other equally, but the eldest always gets blamed.

His brother, Kyle, was 2 years younger than him and hence 4 years younger than me. He looked like a miniature Matt but not as many freckles. When that book, *Freckle Juice,* came out I was sure that someone knew about my cousins, because either one could have been the little boy on the cover. Kyle was always following us around, asking us to let him play. We pretty much used him as a 'go-fetch-it' kid. "Hey Kyle, we need a snack, wanna go get it?" "Hey Kyle, we need some bubbles, wanna go get them?" That sort of thing. Worked out well for us. There was one thing about Kyle that didn't work out so well, he was a world-class snitch! That kid would run and rat us out before we even knew he was watching. He burned us more times than I can count. If we were doing something we shouldn't have been- and more often than not we were - Kyle was always watching us, ready to snitch. When he got old enough to understand the power of information, he went from world-class snitch to world-class blackmailer! I think we actually funded his first dirt bike!

Matt, Kyle, Mia and I became quite a little clique on the block. We played baseball, rode bikes, skateboarded and roller skated. We each had a pool and in the summer we would go from one pool to the next – changing houses only when we had depleted the stash of Dilly bars or Freeze-E-pops in our parents' freezers. If I wasn't at Matt's, I was at Mia's; and if Mia wasn't at my house, she was at Matt's. We were always together in some sort of manner. It was great having such wonderful friends who were so much fun. It was a sweet life and we were very carefree.

Eventually, some of the other houses in our new subdivision started selling and we had more new neighbors and more new friends. Down on the opposite end of our block a tiny, timid girl named Jessi moved in. She was 3 years older than I was – which kind of bummed me out 'cause I was like the block's kingpin up until then. Jessi was short and very thin. She had brown hair that was short all over except for this long piece that hung down the side. She called it a 'tail' and that is what it looked like exactly. We couldn't figure out why a person would want to look like a dog or cat, but Jessi regarded her tail with affection. She started growing it when her cat, Meowcifer, died. We had no idea how long that tail would grow, or why, but she had been growing it for over a year.

Jessi's parents were old. Well, older than all of ours anyway. Her Dad always sat on the front porch in his rocking chair, smoking. He was like the block's watchman. I wondered if he ever went to work? He was always sitting out there. Rocking and smoking; smoking and rocking. As we rode by Jessi's house on our bikes he would nod, take a puff, and rock. Nod, puff, rock. Nod, puff, rock. It was an interesting way to pass the time. Jessi's Mom was one of those 'working' women. My Mom called her a 'feminist' and said she 'didn't know her place.' This confused me a bit, since my Mom always told me I could do whatever I wanted with my life. I suppose Jessi's Mom's ambition was to work at Fairplay grocery store. In any case, she was mostly gone, except in the evenings when she would join Jessi's Dad on the porch. She wasn't a smoker, but she always had a can of a very stinky, foamy drink. We found out years later that it was beer. She apparently was a beer snob, as she only drank the "King" of beers.

Jessi didn't seem to want to spend much time at her house, so she was usually down at mine or Mia's. We assumed it was because of her older brother, Johnny. Johnny was always driving up and down the street in his red, 1979 Mustang. He thought he was so cool. He called us 'pipsqueaks' because he could drive and all us *kids* had to ride our bikes. He would squeal his tires and leave skid marks on the pavement. He had an odd way of dressing too. He would tuck his pants into his socks, wear high topped shoes with the tongues hanging out, a black and red leather jacket, and one - only one- white, glove. Jessi told me it was because his musical idol only wore one glove too.

"Who would only wear one glove?" I asked her one day.

"Who knows, my brother is weird," she replied flatly as if she had given that answer over and over.

Jessi wasn't very athletic like Mia and I were, but she was still fun. When we would go to the large, empty corn field behind our houses to play pitcher, catcher, batter she would sit on the grass and cheer for us. She was the universal cheerleader. I asked her once if she would ever be a real cheerleader and she said, "No way, those girls are twits!"

Our neighborhood gang was completed when a set of girls moved in across the street from me. Their names were Stephanie and Samantha Ferris, and they were real, live twins! They both had blonde hair, blue eyes and were very pretty. Mia's Mom said they were *unnaturally* pretty - like little, porcelain dolls. The sole difference between them was bangs. Stephanie had bangs; Samantha did not. Stephanie said she wanted to be an individual and distinguish herself from her sister. I thought they still looked identical, but it was helpful for telling them apart. We were all very excited to meet them. To us, having the name Ferris automatically made you the coolest kid around, add to that being twins, oh man! Of course, they were no relation to the folks that designed the Ferris wheel, but it was still cool. Steph and Sam's parents were divorced. This was a new term for me, I had no idea

what a "divorcee" was. I quickly found out by
eavesdropping on my parents that a "divorcee" was a
woman who was scorned because her husband
couldn't keep 'it' in his pants. It took me a few years to
figure out what 'it' was – but I think I got the gist of it.
Steph and Sam's Mom tried very hard to be our friend.
She always invited us in for cookies and milk, had us
over for sleepovers, took us to the movies and paid for
all the snacks. As I look back on it, I know she was
trying to buy her daughters' approval, something every
parent has done at one time or another.

I met Mr. Ferris only a few times, and each time was
not under the best circumstances. The first time was
definitely not a good scene. He had come by to see his
daughters unannounced. Apparently, when you are
divorced you need permission to see your kids, and this
day he definitely DID NOT have permission. There was
a lot of yelling – loud yelling – followed by Mrs. Ferris
throwing pots and pans at him as he ran down the
driveway. She had quite an arm! One pot lid skipped
down her driveway like a rock on water and pegged Mr.
Ferris in the butt. It was quite a show – but I felt bad
for Mrs. Ferris; she was crying and he was yelling. This
was the first time I heard the word "fuck" and I believe
it was used in the phrase "You fucking prick!" It took me
even longer to find out what a 'prick' was. I was

disappointed to know that the meaning was essentially the same as 'it.'

Other people moved into our neighborhood over the next year, but no more young kids for us to add to the gang. There were two men who moved in next to Mia's house. They were "friends" and lived together. They had the best landscaped yard on our block. No cookie-cutter house for Mr. Bartlett and Mr. Jonas. They had to be distinct. Mr. Bartlett didn't work and he spent his days planting flowers and plants in their yard. No ordinary lawn gnomes or tacky plastic flamingos for him. Nope. He preferred tiny, perfectly sculpted trees, big, bronze Buddha statues and my favorite thing, the fountain of the woman wearing the bedsheet, holding a bucket that had a place of preference underneath the giant picture window.

Mr. Bartlett was also a theme decorator. He loved to decorate the house for every occasion. On Halloween he put out an assortment of homemade tombstones, ghosts, vampires and scarecrows – and of course, plenty of cottony, white, spider webbing. His house was the spookiest on our block and he loved hearing the *ooohs* and *ahhhs* when we walked by. His friend, Mr. Jonas, didn't seem to care one way or another about the appearance of his home. He was hardly ever there anyway as he worked in the city as a lawyer. I overheard Mia's Mom and Dad talking about how he must be the 'husband' and Mr. Bartlett was the 'wife.' I thought I must have misheard because a *man* couldn't be a *wife* after all. My parents always talked about how odd it was that no women ever came and visited and how strangely Mr. Bartlett walked. I used to think he had a stroke like my Grandpa, because he walked with one hand bent funny.

We didn't care about any of that, Mr. Bartlett was very nice to us. He would let me help plant his flowers; showing me how deep to make the hole, how to add just the right dirt and fertilizer. When it came time for Halloween he would always ask us to help him put out his cemetery stones and place his spiderwebbing.

"Where should Mr. I. M. Bones go?" or "Do you think the bush needs more webs?" he would ask us with a cheery note in his voice.

We really didn't care one way or another, but it was fun to help him get ready for his favorite holiday. Mr. Bartlett told us that Halloween was special to him because he could be anything he wanted on that one day of the year. He always told us to be something outrageous that we would never think of being. Most of us were the typical vampires, witches and ghosts, but I would try to take his advice to heart. I remember being a jockey once – replete with cardboard horse and jockey garb; and a basket of laundry – with socks, underwear and bras stuck all over. I almost always won best costume at my school for my creativity. I owe that to Mr. Bartlett, he did teach me how to access my creative side.

Not everyone enjoyed the creative outpouring of our fancy neighbors. Especially not the Richardsons. They lived right next door to Mr. Bartlett and Mr. Jonas – and they had little tolerance for the 'hokey pokey' decorations. Mr. Richardson was a plumber – and hence a 'man's man.' My mother used to say that he got his education inside a shitter, and hence why he had 'shit for brains.' Mr. Richardson didn't have any kids, and he surely didn't like all of us riding up and down on *his* sidewalk. However, if I wanted to get from my house to Mia's I would have to ride past his house. He would yell and complain that we were getting tire prints on his clean sidewalk. My father pointed out to him once that, "The sidewalk is city property, not personal property."

To which he got the reply, "Screw you," from Mr. Richardson.

Mrs. Richardson sent over some brownies the next day to say, "I'm sorry" for her husband's bad words. She was a very nice and very plump woman. Sometimes we would see her on her front porch

drinking Coke right from the bottle and we would stop
and say hello. She was a very soft-spoken woman,
which didn't surprise me, as her husband was so loud. I
suspect she couldn't get a word in edgewise with him.
She had tightly curled black hair, which she sometimes
put in a net to keep it from blowing all over. Also, she
had the most perfectly defined eyebrows that I had
ever seen. She told Mia and me that she plucked out
her eyebrows just to pencil them back in. What a
ludicrous idea! We both thought she was nuts, and
even more nuts when we tried to pluck just one
eyebrow hair. It hurt like h –e –double toothpicks –
HELL for those of you who don't know - we never did
that again. Well, not until we were older anyway.

The Richardsons got into many heated arguments
with Mr. Bartlett and Mr. Jonas. Especially the first
Valentine's Day when Mr. Bartlett decided to put up a
stone sculpture of a cupid in his front yard. Mr.
Richardson called it 'obscene' and told Mr. Bartlett that
if he didn't remove it, he was gonna be sorry. Mr.
Bartlett tried to reason with him, but Mr. Richardson
was too pig-headed to listen. A few days later we
found the cupid broken into a million pieces on the
front lawn. No one ever accused Mr. Richardson, but
we all knew that he was the one who destroyed the
cupid. Matt wanted to play Columbo and try and find
clues to whom had done the crime, but Mr. Bartlett just

cleaned up his sculpture and never decorated for
Valentine's Day again.

On the corner lot across from my house - and next to
the Ferris' - were the Smiths. Mrs. Smith was a short,
thin woman with long, braided brown hair, and thick,
ugly glasses. She always wore dresses or skirts – never
pants or shorts. She was pregnant when they moved
into the neighborhood, but fell down the stairs and lost
the baby when she was 7 months along. She was a very
sad woman, even before she lost the baby. Mr. Smith
worked at the steel mill with my father. My father used
to say that he was a 'real bastard' and 'meaner than a
dog fightin' over a bone.' He looked mean too. He had
a permanent scowl on his face, especially when we
would ride or walk across his lawn.   Unlike Mr.
Richardson, who was just crotchety, Mr. Smith looked
like he would beat the hell out of you if you looked at
him wrong. We could hear the yelling coming from
their house in the middle of the night, and sometimes
Mrs. Smith would scream. Loud, blood-curdling
screams. Once or twice my father would make his way
over to their house. He never made it past the front
door, Mrs. Smith would talk to him, then send him
away.

When my father would come in, he would say to my Mom in a hushed voice, "He did it again, should we call the police?"

My Mom always said, "I'm not sure honey, do you want to be on his bad side even more than you already are?"

It took only a few months for me to figure out what my Mom and Dad were talking about. Even a 9-year-old could see the black eyes, bruises and scrapes that Mrs. Smith always seemed to have and figure out that a mean husband plus bruises equals trouble. A few months after Mrs. Smith lost her baby she came home in the middle of the afternoon with a cast on her arm. Two falls down the stairs in that short of a time either meant Mrs. Smith was really clumsy, or someone had *helped* her along down the stairs. We felt very bad for her. She was a lonely woman, and always looked at us with a mixture of sadness and fear. It was almost as if she were silently warming us to stay away; I wish someone would have told her to stay away from that mean man.

Of all our new neighbors, the best moved in last. On the end of our block – the far corner – was a vacant lot full of these funny looking trees. They were large trees, but very short – and their branches intertwined every which way. It reminded me of locking fingers. Large, wooden, locking fingers. The base of the trunks were low to the ground, but the tops went up much higher than we could see, and all intertwined as well. The effect was much like a giant, tree canopy. Across the lot from these trees was a small orchard of crabapple trees. Tons and tons of ready-to-throw crabapples! The lot was completely fenced in, so to get to the trees, we would have to climb over the fence. Of course, we were all warned not to ever climb over the fence; but we did it on a daily basis anyway. One day we were on our way over the fence when an official looking man stopped us.

"What do you kids think you are doing going over that fence?" he asked with a very stern tone.

"Listen dude, we go in there all the time and play," Matt said, with his own attempt at a stern tone.

"We are about to start construction on a new house here, so you kids better stay out, could get dangerous in there," the man said, and walked away.

We were all wondering what kind of house they were going to build, who was going to move in, and if they were going to get rid of our trees. We couldn't lose our cool climbing trees or our crabapple fire power!

For the next 6 months there was a lot of commotion on our little block. Construction crews, large excavators, dump trucks, cement trucks, contractors. It was a nosey child's dream! While our parents did nothing but complain about the dust and the noise, we kids found it totally fascinating. We would sit across the street and watch all the workers. Sometimes we would venture over and try to find out what was going on. They were uninterested in our comments, and most of the time told us to 'beat it' – sometimes with not so nice words. I have to admit, construction workers have very colorful vocabularies! We watched as most, not all, of the crabapple trees were removed, and a big hole was built for the foundation of the house. We sat there day after day watching them take tree after tree away. At the end of the tear-down period most of the crabapple trees were gone, but luckily all the 'finger-locking' trees were still there.

The house that was built on this lot was absolutely huge. It was not like the brick bungalow houses that adorned the rest of the block. No, this house looked like it belonged in the country on many acres of farmland. Three floors of beautiful, deep red brick with stunning bright white accents towered over the other houses on the block – making it easily twice as large as any other house. A full wrap-around porch held up by white, wooden columns encircled the home with country charm, just waiting for people to sit and gossip with a glass of iced tea. The large windows had these white crossbars on them, which made the house look like something out of a Charles Dickens novel. In the backyard there was a large 'barn' looking building, painted in matching red. We weren't sure if it was a garage or a barn, but it had matching white trim as well. Our childhood imaginations concocted theories that the new owner was a mad scientist and he was going to have his laboratory out back. We started imaging that he would steal up the children from the neighborhood and commence evil experiments on them. Matt was sure the new owner was going to keep animals in there – it did look like a barn after all – but my Aunt told him that we lived in a 'residential' area, and no livestock could be kept here.

A long driveway went up to the barn / garage / evil scientist lab. There were some trees left around the property, which framed the house in green foliage. The land to the left of the house was cleared – except for about 6 crabapple trees and our climbing trees. When the house was finished, we all stood looking at it and wondering who would be moving in.

"Who needs that much room?" my Mom asked Mrs. Ferris one evening during their weekly Bunco game.

"I don't know, but it sure is a lot of house and a lot of barn," she replied.

"Perhaps they have some sort of business," suggested my aunt, "or it is going to be an inn or something."

"God, I hope not," replied my Mom, "that would mean strangers coming and going all year round. I don't like the idea of strangers being on our block, makes me worry about the kids' safety, you know?"

"I guess we will just have to wait and see who, exactly, moves in," said Mia's Mom as she announced another Bunco.

As Mia, Matt, Steph, Samantha and I sat and listened to this conversation while playing Space Invaders on my brand-new Atari, we, too, were wondering the same things, but we had another motive. We wanted to know if we would be able to climb our trees any longer. In our innocent, child lives, losing our playground would have been totally devastating. Little did we understand then, how unimportant climbing in a tree really is in the scope of bigger things.

Chapter 2

My reminiscing about our new mysterious neighbor was brought to a screeching halt by a hard tug on my jacket. I peer down to see my youngest son, Ryan, who is looking up at me with questioning eyes. He is only 10, and all this hub-bub about Mommy's old neighborhood was probably not the least bit interesting to him. My eldest son, Mark, who has brought me back *here* by his actions, stands cross-armed and defensive, his eyes saying what his mouth knows he better not, 'this sucks and what is the point?' Typical 15-year-old ignorance. He knows *everything* about *everything*. So did I. He has experienced a lifetime in his 15 years and no one can or had better tell him how to live *his* life. He doesn't need me or my words of so-called wisdom 'cause he knows it all and is not afraid to tell anyone who will listen how 'smart' and 'all-knowing' he is. Oh, how I remember that feeling. Self-righteousness blended with ignorance and inexperience. The formula for youth. Thinking, and truly believing, that you know better than anyone else. It is a virtuous place to live in – until someone evicts you and throws you on your ass!

How did this happen? How did I raise a son who is so cut-off from me? I swore that I would not be unavailable or uninterested in the lives of my children.

My husband and I promised to be that perfect mixture
of good parent and friend. We were going to do what
no other parent on the face of the Earth could do – be
the EVERYparent. Have children who were obedient,
smart, fun, creative. We were going to be the hip, cool,
trendy, yuppy parents who had everything and could do
it all.

Apparently, my childhood all-knowingness didn't
carry over into my adult life – because I was totally
blindsided to find out my son was practically a drop out,
was smoking pot – *marijuana at 15 years old* - skips
school and goes to his friends' houses to 'party' all day
while their parents are at work. He even took the
midtown bus on his own in the middle of the school day
to meet some of these 'friends' downtown. I shudder
to think of what could have happened to him on his day
of free reign. I was probably 20 before I took any bus
anywhere! Furthermore, I am petrified of what could
happen if his behavior escalates. He is only 15 – I fear
for what he will do at 16. I am not prepared – what
parent is – to handle these issues. How do you tell that
'all knowing' child that he is wrong, his actions are
wrong, he is putting himself in danger? My husband
and I wracked our brains trying to find a solution to this
dilemma. We tried every avenue to no avail. Finally, I
knew what I had to do.

Looking over at my boys now I have a powerful urge to protect them. I want to take them and just run away from this place and never reveal the reason why I have brought them here. Remembering is not something I really want to do. It is not something that I, or any of my fellow neighborhood mates, ever wanted to do again. Our parents moved us all away from this place for good reason. We vowed to ourselves and to each other never to talk about what happened here. Our parents were surely not going to mention it. Moving to new, peaceful subdivisions in various states would make all the bad memories go away. I now baptize you *free and clear* by virtue of your new address. Bullshit. My mind can never forget and not one, single, day goes by when I don't remember it – all of it.

Chapter 3

"Earth to Mom......HELL-looo!!," Mark shouts at me. "I want to leave this ghetto-riffic place and go get some food." Mark is extremely disrespectful. His attitude always reminds my Mom of me as a child. I didn't see myself as disrespectful then, but now I realize that I surely was.

"Uh, Mom...can we just go or what? I don't give a rat's ass about who lived where on your block as a kid. What does this have to do with me skipping school? Is this sort of punishment? Do I have to see how rough you had it as a child and how far you and Dad have come? I get it now. I am grateful Mom, thanks for everything. *Really.* I am so, so grateful. Can we get some Taco Bell now?" Mark rambles on and on with that *I- don't- really- care- sarcastic- to- the- core tone* that has become so commonplace for him.

"Is that what you think this is about Mark?" I ask him. "Do you think this is a punishment?"

"Well yeah, why else would you bring us to the ghetto and spend an hour talking about all your old friends. There has to be a reason for all this. I figure, show me how you lived and then I will be grateful for the life I have. Show me your small, gross house and I will be grateful for all those things I have. Remember,

25

Mom, I am so, so spoiled. You tell me all the time. I agree, I am so spoiled. I love my house. Can we freakin' go now?"

I am amazed at my son's stupidity. Not only is he not looking around and seeing that this is an *old* neighborhood, but he clearly is not listening to what I have been telling him. He listens but does not hear. Either that or the pot has already killed too many brain cells.

"Mark, I told you, when I lived here, this was a new neighborhood, new houses, new development. It only looks like this *now*. All these years later. These were nice houses when I lived here. In fact, they were some of the nicest in town."

"So, what is the point then Mom, I would really like to know why we are here," Mark says, with a hint of curiosity in his tone that he can't hide. Perhaps he will become receptive to my lesson. Perhaps when he hears what I have to say – really *hears* it – he will understand.

"Mom, I am hungry too. Can we get some food now?" asks Ryan without the slightest idea of what is going on here.

I decided to bring him along too, as a sort of forced intervention for his future actions. He idolizes his big brother and wants to be just like him – even if being 'him' means getting into trouble. My husband and I decided that even though he is still young the information was worth having. We knew it would probably affect him in a much different manner than Mark, but it might fend off any negative behaviors and help to frame his mode of thinking before things got out of hand.

"Oh Ry, can you wait just a little longer, Mommy wants to finish her story?"

"Come on Mom, we are both starving, there has to be a place we can eat in this dump....er, I mean this lovely town you used to live in," Mark says trying to feign interest in all of this.

I cannot believe the attitude my son is displaying here. Suspended from school, practically failing – you would think that he would welcome any type of activity that didn't involve being grounded to his room without the luxury of his Nintendo Wii or his PlayStation 3. But no, here he is with even more attitude, if it were possible, and no interest in hearing what I have to say. It is sad, really, to have a child who is that far disconnected. A child who truly believes that he or she is above any type of life lesson.

I started to doubt whether this little trip down memory lane was going to make an impact on him at all. Would he really understand the significance of this lesson and take it to heart? Or, would he be true to Mark fashion and ignore everything I have to say and just pretend to be interested. I knew if this didn't' reach him and make him realize that his actions of late were truly world-class stupid, then not much else would register with him. Keeping him safe was no longer something I felt I had control over – he had taken the wheel and he was driving fast toward self- destruction. It is a truly helpless feeling when you realize that your children are mobile and want to get as far from you as they possibly can. While they are running from you, you are running after them – and much can happen during the race. It was my goal to protect my children, in any way I could.

I suppose the time had come to stop sheltering them so much. My husband and I had always been very overprotective parents. Wanting to know the who, what, when, where, why and how long to every move of our children. I think Mark was about 6 years old before we would let him cross the street without holding our hands – and we would still watch him cross. Just to ride his bike he needed a helmet, elbow and knee pads. He wasn't allowed in anyone's pools until he had 3 years of swimming lessons. While his friends were riding their bikes to school, we were still following him in the car. Before either of our boys were allowed to play at anyone's house without one of us present it was a virtual FBI check to have the privilege of watching one of our precious children. Was it a little over the top? Looking back, sure, it was. At the time it felt like it was what we needed to do. Perhaps being the helicopter parents is what made Mark run so fast and furious to his own kind of freedom. Maybe the dope smoking and the bad decisions were a band aid to the suffocation he felt from us?

In retrospect, I think that our tight leash on Mark caused him to run as fast and as far from our tightening grip as soon as he figured out how. He became an expert liar and bullshitter before he was 7 years old. He knew what we wanted to hear, and he was really proficient at convincing us. As our grip loosened, he took more and more liberties with our freedoms. Would it have made any difference if we had this conversation earlier – perhaps a few years ago? I am not really sure, but, I wasn't going to let my fear of revisiting this ugly chapter in my life prevent me from at least trying to make a difference in the outcome of my children's lives. There are just too many unanswered questions about the future, and I wasn't going to let a possible answer slip on by.

Chapter 4

As I look away from my old house, I notice Mark is walking down the street, away from our car – and away from me.

"Hey, where do you think you are going?" I yell to him.

"To get food, I told you, I am starving!"

Apparently, I could not attempt to reason with a hungry child. I hit the alarm button on our SUV and told Ryan to get in and get buckled up. I started the car, did a 3-point turn and headed down the street. Pulling up next to Mark, I opened the window and gently approached him.

"Honey, let's go get something to eat, and then we can come back, and I can finish telling you what we drove 8 hours for me to tell you."

"No thanks Mom. I am done with the little life lesson. I am convinced there is nothing you can tell me that will make any difference. I am a bad kid. I know it, you know it. Let's just drop the crap and get back home so Dad can punish me and you can send me off to military school."

Oh, how I remember the not-so-subtle attempts at reverse psychology with my parents. Telling them that I thought I was a 'bad' child, so they would hurry up and say, 'no honey, you are a great kid,' and hence prove the point I wanted to make: that I didn't deserve to be punished. Mark is so much like me it is scary. Unfortunately, being like me in this world is only going to cause him hurt as people are much less tolerant of belligerent children.

"Mark, get in the car, you shouldn't be walking around here alone, you don't know where you are going."

"Hey, there's an idea. I can get abducted and someone else can raise me. Since I am sooooo much trouble for you and Dad!"

With this ridiculous notion I slammed on the breaks, put the car in park and got out. Ryan was watching me carefully from his seat, apparently afraid to comment.

"Mark, you get your smug ass into this car this instant," I yelled at him, in a tone that I truly try not to use unless the situation is one that warrants it.

Mark, realizing that I meant business, quickly got in and buckled up. As I turned to get into the car I noticed where I was parked. I was in front of the old

Delaney house. The Delaneys lived two doors down from Jessi and they were very, very odd people. They were one of the last families to move into the neighborhood and it was under the strangest circumstances. The 'SOLD' sign on the front yard alerted us that the last home had finally sold, and everyone on the block was anxious to see who would move in. One night, at approximately 11:30 pm, the moving vans came idling down the street. Under the cloak of darkness, the Delaneys were moving in. No one saw this nocturnal activity except Jessi, who had heard the movers speaking Spanish, and got up to look out her window. She said the truck was filled with odd things – big, colorful, pink, blue and red garbage bag looking things, huge fish tanks, about a hundred desk lamps, a box that said "waterbed," lots of mirrors, black furniture and something that looked a lot like a coffin. Jessi said it was the oddest assortment of things she had ever seen go into a house.

The Delaneys didn't arrive at their new house for almost a week. The neighborhood practically became a grapevine of gossip regarding the new neighbors. Finally, the first glimpse of the Delaneys brought every busy-body from the neighborhood out to "water" their front lawns. They pulled up at 8:00 at night in a bright, blue mini-van. The mother exited the car first. Mrs. Delaney had long – and I mean long – blonde hair. She was thin and wore a tie-dyed dress. Her 3-year-old daughter, Star, had long, long brown hair and wore a similar tie-dyed ensemble. Mr. Delaney was lanky – eerily lanky. He wore faded blue jeans and a bright pink shirt. His hair was almost as long as Mrs. Delaney's, but held back in a ponytail. When Jessi's father waved at him from his spot on the front porch, Mr. Delaney stuck up his hand in this odd gesture and replied, "Peace man." Yes, they were very odd people.

My Mother told Mia's Mom that the Delaney's were going to be trouble, she was part psychic after all, or at least she pretended to be.

"Mark my words Mary, those people are going to be the blemish on the skin of this neighborhood!"

Her reply was, "I thought hippies were supposed to be all about love and peace and groovy things?"

"Sure, groovy things like beer, bongs and funky music. I am keeping my kids away from their house, they may get a contact high!"

The truth was, the Delaneys were no trouble at all. They were very friendly, always said 'hi' and waved. They barely left their house. I guess Mr. Delaney didn't work because he was always home – and so was Mrs. Delaney. They sure had a lot of friends though; people were always coming and going from that house. Sometimes, in the summer when the windows were open, I could hear the music all the way to my house. My Mom said it was 'the devil's music,' and she would shut my windows. I kind of liked the music, actually, except when it woke me up in the middle of the night. The Delaneys had no sense of time. They had that music playing all night long. Matt started conspiring that they were a family of vampires, who had moved in during the dark of night and slept all day. He suggested to us that if we broke into their house we would find them all sleeping in coffins. Matt was weird with all his conspiracy theories, but this one started making sense to us after a while. I mean, what type of person never comes out of their house before dusk? Jessi reminded us that she thought she saw a coffin-like table going into the house. It was all very strange.

"HONKKKKKKKKKKK, HONKKKKKKKKKKKKKKKKKKK! MOM, are you COMING or WHAT?" the blaring honk of my horn blasted me from my Delaney flashback. I got into the car, buckled up, turned into the Delaney's driveway – or whomever lived there now – and headed down the street to find my boys some food.

"Mark, why do you insist on being such a brat today?" I asked my son who was brooding in the seat next to me.

"I don't know Mom. I don't know much of anything apparently. All I know for sure is I am really, really ready to go home," came the answer that sounded more truthful than anything he has said to me in months.

As I looked around for a place where we could sit down and eat, I was starting to doubt my decision to bring my boys here. Self-doubt is one of my best qualities. I am a pro at the self- doubt. I didn't used to be that way, in fact, I used to be the exact opposite. Something about having children and being responsible for a life not your own has caused me to doubt and re-examine every decision I have made since my boys were born. From whether to breast or bottle feed to where to send them to school – every decision became a marathon battle of my opinion or thought versus my husband's. No decision could be made alone and, "Well honey, what do you think," became my new mantra. Heaven forbid we disagree, that decision would take a year to finalize. Yep, self-doubt was definitely on my list of major character flaws.

I was even beginning to doubt that I would find a suitable restaurant in this neighborhood, but finally, I see the glowing yellow "M" in the distance that signifies my temporary reprieve from badly behaved children. McDonald's it is, and no one had better complain.

As soon as Ry spots the golden arches his order comes spewing from his mouth, "Oh, Mom, can I get the cheeseburger happy meal with no pickles, with a chocolate shake?"

"I hate frickin' MCDs," was murmured from the slouching figure sitting next to me.

"Well, this is going to be it boys, we will get a more substantial dinner later at the hotel," I remind them.

"God damn it Mom, do we really have to stay in this cesspool of a town for a whole night?"

"Mark, if I have to tell you one more time not to use that language - especially in front of your brother – you *will* be going off to military school!"

Having pulled the military school card just one too many times, Mark looked at me with eyes that said, "yeah, sure," although he didn't dare say it. His language has been getting worse and worse as of late, and in fact I can't believe he pulls out the foul words as much as he does. If I had said 'God Damn' to my mother or father….well, let's just say I wouldn't be sitting down for quite some time. I distinctly recall a time when my mother had grounded me for sneaking off to Mia's house instead of doing my homework. When she told me I was grounded I responded, "Screw you!" My father was in the living room, heard me say this to my Mom and came quickly into the kitchen.

"What did you just say to your Mother?" came the firm tone at least 2 octaves lower than his normal speech that suggested I better not mess with him.

Being ever so defiant this particular evening, I answered, "None of your business."

My father reached out to grab me, but I bolted down our steps and out into the backyard. I quickly ran past our pool, under our swing set and flipped myself right over our back gate with the agility of a gymnast. I would have given it a 10.0 easily. The German judge maybe a 9.5 because my foot touched the top of the fence. My father was only a few feet behind me, but of course, he couldn't catch me. So, I stood there, arms crossed in a very self-satisfied manner, thinking that I had won. My Father, who was a very wise man without much of a sense of humor, just looked at me and said, "That's OK, you have to come home sometime." He turned and walked back to the house. I knew I was the one who was screwed. As I went from friend to friend, each one telling me that they couldn't let me in, I knew that my Dad had activated the "Code Blue" phone tree, instructing each of my friends' parents not to allow me sanctuary. Within an hour I was home and grounded.

As we walked into the brightly lit McDonald's dining room, I was more determined than ever that I had to continue with my intervention, but I needed to think about how to proceed. I knew if I went about it the wrong way, Mark would tone me out and it would all be for nothing. I couldn't risk losing my son – perhaps both of them. I decided to let them eat, calm down and recharge. Then I would take them back and try to make them see – and to do that, I would have to see again myself.

Chapter 5

There they stand - the finger-locking trees. It is if no time has passed. They are exactly the same as they were in my youth, as well as they are in my nightmares. Granted, the land around the trees is much different. The lot is now full of garbage, empty beer cans, plastic bags that have caught themselves on the spidery limbs of the spiny bushes, waving like ragged pirate-ship flags. But the trees remain the same. Sturdy, stately, tall, green. It is almost as if all the destruction and vandalism on this block stopped right at the tree line. These trees are representative of life – the life that goes on – even in the midst of chaos.

Sitting in my SUV at the end of my old block with my boys, it was if I was watching a movie of myself playing as a child on this lot of trees. The memories are so vivid. Our little gang spent day after day after day down on this corner. We climbed the trees, had crabapple fights, looked for crawfish in the dirty, disgusting ditch that ran behind the property. There was always something fun to do down here. Even though it was only at the end of our block, it seemed miles away from our houses. We could pretend to be anything here. The trees were truly magical –their branches transforming instantly into a horse or a motorcycle; a spaceship or a racecar. We could be anything we wanted in the sanctuary of our tree play yard.

I turn my attention to the house – which is a mere shadow of what it used to be. The vibrant brick has already faded to a dull, muddy color; the porch is in bad disrepair, the roof is half gone. Many, if not most, of the windows are boarded up and the barn was torn down years ago. The yard itself is overgrown with weeds. Not a hint of the beautiful estate that was built here not so many years ago. It seems unreal that this property is so badly neglected, but then again, so is the rest of the neighborhood. The crabapple trees are long gone, bull dozed and discarded. The lot is now once again encased in fencing – but not because of new development, but because of dangerous disrepair.

In its new stages, this house used to be truly magnificent. Bright, vibrant - full of life and hope. It was amazing even to us kids. As the construction came to a close, we were eagerly waiting to see who would move in. Who would build such a large house on our little block? All the speculation about the owner finally came to an end on May 23rd, 1981. I remember this date only because it happened to be my birthday, my tenth birthday to be exact. My friends and I were on the front lawn, chucking a big stick at a donkey piñata my Mom had hung from our tree. In mid swipe Mia noticed the moving vans. Three, large moving vans were parked at the end of the block. There were men hurriedly carrying boxes and furniture from the vans into the house. In a matter of a few hours, all three vans were empty and had moved away. All that remained on the long driveway was a blue car. Someone was there, and we couldn't wait to find out who.

Sitting in my front yard having birthday cake, Mia, Matt, Steph, Sam, Jessi and I were trying to decide how we were going to find out who lived there. It was a total obsession. First, find out who lives there; second, find out if we could still climb on the trees. We finally settled on our infamous coupon scam. Over the summer, in an attempt to get money to go the local Dairy Queen, I had come up with the totally brilliant – and yet equally illegal – scheme of taking the free coupon packs out of our unsuspecting neighbors' mailboxes, stapling them together and selling them back at the price of $1.00 a pack. I am quite sure many of our neighbors realized our scam, but most paid the $1.00 anyway. Except for the Delaneys. Mr. Delaney muttered something about coupons being "Payment for the money-grubbing, inflation causing ' man'" and how "Food should be given to the people or we should grow our own."

We sold his pack to Jessi's Mom, who remarked that, "These are the same coupons we use at Fairplay." All in total we had made $15.00 off the free coupons we got in the mail. That bought a lot of Mr. Mistys and Dilly Bars.

In any case, we decided to use the same concept as an excuse to ring the doorbell and see who would answer. We would introduce ourselves as the friendly neighborhood kids, ask him or her to buy our fundraising coupons and then happen to mention that we liked climbing in those trees. It was all rehearsed and official.

Wasting no time, we forged up our coupon pack and headed down the block. My heart was thumping. I never realized how important those stupid trees were – or how damn nosey we all were – until we started obsessing about finding out who lived on the far corner of our block. We walked slowly up onto the large front porch, up to the door, and rang the bell. As I looked behind me I was disgusted to see that my fellow comrades had fallen back in retreat, and had left me as the sole representative of our coupon enterprise.

"Coming. Just a minute," came a voice from inside the house.

This was it, I was going to meet the lucky owner of this new house.

"Hi there. Can I help you?"

She was totally not what I was expecting. A short, thin, older woman had come to the door. She had gray hair – tightly rolled in 'old lady perm' style – wire rimmed glasses, a soft, wrinkled face, she was wearing an apron and smelled like cookies.

My God, Mrs. Claus had moved in on our block!

She was totally the grandma type. In that moment I thought, *Yes, this is exactly who should live in this house, she matches it.*

"Honey, are you OK?" she asked me, as I was standing there in sort of a freeze frame.

"Oh, I am sorry. Hello there. My name is Kayla, and I am selling coupons for……for my Brownie troop, would you like to buy a pack, they are just a dollar?"

"Sure honey, let me run and get some money for you. I can always use some coupons," she said, smiling and giving me a very warm, fuzzy feeling.

As she walked away from the door, my cohorts bounded up the stairs to see what I had found out.

"So, what's the deal, is she gonna let us climb the trees," Mia asked cutting to the chase.

Come on Kayla, let us in, what is she like? Is she old? Mean? Nice," Stephanie interrupts.

"Does she look like a mad scientist," Matt asked.

"Well hello there children? Are all of you in the brownie troop?" the nice lady asked, looking amused at our discussion.

"Hey, lady, I am a *boy*, I am not a brownie or any other kind of dessert," my cousin said with manly pride well beyond his years.

"Certainly sir," the nice lady responded, giving Matt a little bow. Listen, I was looking over my yard, and thought that those trees over there might make good climbing trees. Since I have no plans on climbing them, I thought I would let you know if you would like, you are more than welcome to. I just ask that you leave the crabapple trees alone, don't climb on them," she said, clearly having overheard our conversation.

"Thanks so much Ms. – er – thanks," I said as I handed her the coupon pack, now a bit of guilt hitting me for scamming this very nice lady.

"Mrs. Maloney is the name sweethearts, come visit me anytime." With that, she turned and closed the door.

We were thrilled beyond belief! We hadn't lost our trees. We immediately ran over and began climbing them. Once we were all up and settled in our favorite roosts, we decided that we should name our little tree hideaway place something, so that we could say, 'Hey you, meet me at.....' and we alone would be able to decipher the meaning. Naming it was another story. Proper names certainly wouldn't work, much to Stephanie's dismay. "Meet me at Fred" didn't have much of a ring. Planets didn't work either, so Matt's suggestion of "Pluto" or "Mars" wasn't cutting it. Mia suggested "eert" which was tree spelled backwards. Clever, but it was hard to say and sounded too much like fart.

While we were thinking of our name, I suggested we play one of our favorite games – left to right. We would start on the far-left tree, climb up and try to make it all the way to the right tree without climbing back down. There were 4 trees in a row, but the branches all intertwined. So, if you figured out the right way to go, sort of like in a maze, you could go from left to right. As I was explaining the game, Jessi got very excited.

"I know the name, I know the name!" she shouted. "My father had a boat once and he took me out sailing a few times. He told me that on a boat, left is "starbort" and right is "port" – or vice versa. Anyway, since you can go from the left to the right on these trees, I think that is the perfect name!"

"Starbort and Port. I like it," I said.

"Up for a vote then," Mia suggested. "All in favor, say 'I.'"

We all said 'I' and our little group of finger locking trees affectionately became 'Starbort and Port'.

Chapter 6

"That is the stupidest name for a hideout that I have ever heard," Mark sneered, "and isn't it starboard," he asked with arrogant self-satisfaction.

I hardly expected him to understand or care about my old tree play yard. Talking about these trees and what we did here were just a means to an end. I decided as long as I was going to take the trip down memory lane I had better make it a long trip. Truth be told, I was having a good time remembering the *good* times that happened here, on this block. Far too much of my time and energy has been devoted to recalling the bad things. It was high time I pay homage to the happy times I enjoyed with my best friends. That was who they were – all of them – my best friends. We were tighter than any group of friends could be. All of us, different ages, different ideals, different families – but all friends.

"Mommy, what did you do down here besides climbing trees?" Ry asked me, obviously with more genuine interest than my eldest son had.

"Oh Ryan, you wouldn't believe the fun we had down here," I exclaimed, trying to boost their interest. "We came down here every day. We climbed the trees, ran around and played tag, did daredevil things, had crabapple fights, made forts – there was always something to do at Starbort and Port.

That was the truth of it. Never a day went by when we played outside that one- or any assortment of us- didn't come down to the corner lot to play. For us, tree climbing was a way to escape reality. Not that our realities were something we needed escaping from, we just enjoyed being hidden up in the branches, away from the world. Usually, no one knew we were even there. Except Mrs. Maloney, of course, because she would hear us coming.

Mrs. Maloney would often sit on her big porch and wave to us as we rode our bikes down to her lot. Sometimes she would even give us cookies or snacks and freshly squeezed lemonade.

She would always say, "You haven't had lemonade 'till you have had homemade lemonade while sitting on a country porch."

This seemed true, but we definitely weren't in the country. I guess Mrs. Maloney built that big ole' house so she could pretend to be in the country.

We found out over the next year that Mrs. Maloney was a widow, which meant her husband had died and went to heaven. He had a heart attack and died young, but left Mrs. Maloney with a nice sum of money.

She told us, "I loved my Henry, more than anything, but his passing did me some good."

We were confused as to how her husband dying did her good, but we continued to listen to the story anyway. Apparently, they had gotten married when she was only 16 years old. She said she had not experienced life yet. They had 5 children and she was a Mom and a housewife for 35 years. That was her "calling."

"When my Henry died I knew what he would have wanted. He would have wanted me to start to embrace my real self. Do the activities that being a dedicated Mom and wife prohibited me from doing. So that is what I am doing. I bought me this house, I have an art studio in the barn, and I am going to begin nurturing my artistic side."

So that was what was in the barn! An art studio. We asked Mrs. Maloney if we could go see what was in the barn, but she told us she wasn't ready to reveal her art. Someday she would let us see, but now was not the right time.

Telling us that we couldn't or shouldn't do something was inadvertently like saying, "I double dog dare you to do it." As I said previously, we were badly behaved children. Mrs. Maloney telling us we couldn't look was our invitation to sneak into her barn and see. After we left Starbort and Port, we went to Mia's and staged our plan. We knew that there were windows in the barn, so we decided to try and sneak in through one of the rear ones. We would have to do it late at night, because Mrs. Maloney was a night owl, often baking cookies and cakes into the wee hours of the morning. If I spent the night at Mia's on Friday, it would be easy for us to sneak out. Friday night was Bunco night, and all our parents would be otherwise engaged. Our Moms playing Bunco, drinking a very bitter grape juice; our Dads watching television and drinking Pepsi-colored drinks that burned when you swallowed them! I found that out accidentally once when I thought I was sneaking a sip of my Dad's diet Pepsi. When my Dad realized that I had taken a swig via the rather shocked look on my face, he just chuckled and said, "That'll put hair on your chest!" I thought, *ewwww, I sure don't want hair on my chest*.

So, no problem, we would just sneak out the back door, over her fence, down to the corner and voila! – we can sneak into the barn!

Friday night things were going perfectly as planned. Our parents were playing Bunco and Mia and I easily snuck out. We found ourselves in Mrs. Maloney's yard minutes later and were ready to see what all this art was about. We moved to the rear of the barn and noticed that the windows were quite high. There were garbage cans against the side wall of the barn; we got one and quietly brought it over to stand on. Mia was much smaller than I, so I suggested she get up on the can and try to open the window. Perched precariously up on top, she tried to lift the window; it wouldn't budge.

"Damn thing is locked," she whispered down to me. "But hey, I can see in anyway, there is a light on in there. All I see is a bunch of sheets."

"Sheets? Why would there be sheets in there," I asked myself as much as Mia.

I decided I had to get up to see for myself, so I hoisted myself up onto the can with Mia and peered in. She was right, there were sheets draped all over tall, short, and oddly shaped things. Looked like a festival of mis-shapened ghosts. Satisfied that there was nothing more to see, I started to lower myself down from the can, but Mia had started to do the same. Grave mistake! We both came tumbling down off the can and the can went rolling – LOUDLY – hitting the side of the barn. The neighborhood dogs started to bark, alerting each other that something was amiss and sounding the doggy block alarm. Soon, the entire neighborhood would know someone was doing something that they shouldn't.

"Oh CRAP!" I yelled to Mia. "Let's beat it out of here!"

We ran back to the rear of the yard, hopped the fence and headed toward Mia's house. As we rounded the bend, we saw Mrs. Maloney out on her back porch with a flashlight. She would surely know that someone was out there. Our flawless plan was not so flawless apparently.

Arriving back at Mia's, we were both sore from our topple off the garbage cans. Mia had mud all down the side of her jeans and I had leaves and garbage in my hair. We looked disheveled, and more importantly, guilty. We snuck back inside, down the stairs and into Mia's room.

"Darn, that was a close one," Mia said to me. She looked tremendously relieved.

"Yeah, I know it. We need to keep our noses out of trouble."

"I second that. Pinky swear not to tell anyone that we fell off the cans and into the mud."

"Pinky swear," I replied as we locked our pinkies, winked and hugged. It was now an official secret. The rest of the gang would only know that there were mysterious sheets in the barn, but not how we know or what happened after we found out.   At least we were bringing back information.

Chapter 7

The next morning, while sitting on our favorite roosts at Starbort and Port, Mia and I reported to the rest of the gang about our mission. Speculation about what the sheets were covering – or more precisely, hiding – was running rampant. Everyone had their theories, but Matt's was the most outrageous as usual.

"I know what they are," he announced, "she *is* a mad scientist, and under the sheets are bodies that she is cutting and sewing together. When the moon is full, she will take off the sheets and the light from the moon will bring them back to life. We will have zombies walking all over our block!"

"Matt, you twit, have you been watching too much television or what?" Sam replied. She didn't enjoy anything spooky or scary. In fact, Halloween was a nightmare for her. She was afraid to open the door for the trick-or-treaters because she didn't know who anyone was. A realist at heart, any bending of reality for the purpose of scaring her was simply uncool.

"Oh, scaredy cat Sam, I forgot you don't like ZOMBIES and GHOOOOLIES," Matt taunted.

"Shut up Matt, or you'll be sorry," Stephanie came to the defense of her sister.

"Make me!"

With that, the fight was on! Stephanie ran to the nearest crabapple tree, plucked a crabapple and hurled it right at Matt, nearly missing his head. Matt, refusing to let Steph get the best of him, grabbed an apple off the ground and threw it at her, hitting her square in the stomach.

"Ouch, that hurts," Stephanie whined. Pretending to double over in pain, she grabbed an apple and threw it at Matt, but missed and hit me right in the face!

"Oh now you are all gonna get it, you know I am the best thrower of all of you," I yelled, picking up some mushy apples from the ground and hurling them at anything that moved.

Crabapple fights happened often between us – and they were a lot of fun. Mushy apples were the best because they didn't hurt when you got hit, but they sure made a big mess! Our parents frequently shook their heads at us when we came home – again – covered in smelly apple guts.

We were all into the fight now – the six of us throwing apples at each other and laughing. In the middle of our privately made mayhem, one of Mia's apples sailed by my head, into the street and smacked a car right on the windshield!

"You just nailed my brother's car," Jessi yelled, as Johnny slammed on his brakes.

"Uh oh," Mia squealed, as she scurried up the nearest tree.

"You little pipsqueaks, you hit my car," Johnny yelled as he ran right toward us. "Who threw it, who threw that apple?" he asked, obviously very angry!

Mia, now in the safety zone of the top of the trees, yelled down, "I did, you one-glove wearing loser!"

Johnny looked up into the trees and saw Mia up on one of the highest branches. He tried to get up into the tree to get her, but couldn't hoist himself up. The brilliant thing about our special trees was that they seemed to be made just for kids. The creases and crevices were small and precise, and it took a great deal of dexterity to get up to the highest points. She was safe – and she knew it.

"I'll get you when you come down, twerp," Johnny yelled at her.

Mia just flipped him the bird and laughed. Johnny walked back to his idling Mustang, got in and drove down the block to his house, squealing his tires as he went.

Immediately, Jessi fell to the ground laughing hysterically! She was rolling around snorting. "That was the funniest thing I have ever seen. Oh Mia, you have got to do that again!"

Mia was making her way back down the tree now, looking self-satisfied and smug. She knew she had escaped easily, and this gave her an idea.

"Hey guys, I have an idea for a new game. What if we threw apples at some of the cars that came around the corner and then ran up a tree to escape? Most people wouldn't even know what hit them. Whoever gets the best hit without getting caught gets a free Mr. Misty from DQ courtesy of the rest of us!"

This idea, as ludicrous as it sounded, seemed the *epitome* of *awesome* to us. Not one of us thought that this might be dangerous, cause an accident – or, at the very least – get us into big trouble. No, in our delinquent minds this was the best game ever and we couldn't wait to play. Remember, badly behaved kids.

We set up some ground rules. First, the apple had to be mushy, we didn't want to break a windshield; second, we had to stand by the tree line to throw (which was roughly 45 feet from the street), we didn't want to be too close; third, no one would rat out who actually threw the apple, we wanted to protect each other through group denial; and fourth, the winner would be determined by Jessi who wouldn't play. She had no arm for throwing and knew she wouldn't even make it to the street.

We selected our apples and waited. The beauty was, our play yard was on the corner of a one-way turn. If you went down our block toward the corner, you would have to go around the turn to the left, heading toward the main road. Conversely, if cars came from the main road they could only round the corner to the right and head down our block. Either scenario resulted in cars passing directly in front or our tree haven. We decided that it was too risky to take aim on the cars coming down our block, as it could be one of our parents, so we waited for a car to turn off the main road.

The bad thing about our plan was that there wasn't much traffic on our little block. It took the better part of a half hour for a car to finally turn of the main road and head in our direction. The first car was a bright yellow station wagon. Matt took aim, threw and hit the wagon square in the rear quarter panel. We all ran up into the trees, but no one got out of the car. The driver just opened his window, looked back toward the rear of his car, and sped off.

"Well, that was anti-climactic," Mia said, obviously upset that Matt's hit and score didn't elicit a better response.

"I can do better than that for sure," Mia boasted.

She picked up a large, mushy apple and got into pitcher's stance. In just a few minutes a green Dodge started rounding the curve. Mia was ready and as soon as the car was within throwing distance she threw – and missed by a mile – the car slowed down, but did not stop. Mia was pissed at herself, as she was sure she could win.

"Oh sure, when I am aiming for Kayla I can hit the car, but when I try, I miss!"

"I guess it will be up to me," I announced as I picked up my apple.

I was ready to get this game over with. We waited and waited until finally a car rounded the turn. It was a bright blue, two-seater sports car. I got into position and as soon as the car rounded the corner I threw and – BAM – a direct hit right on the driver's window! Perfect hit! I was looking forward to my lime green Mr. Misty already!

The car screeched to a halt and we all high-tailed it to the trees! This driver was none too happy about having his car riddled with apple guts, he got out and started walking briskly toward us. All safely up in the trees, we expected no trouble. We were wrong.

"Hey, which one of you kids threw an apple at my car?" the guy yelled. He was young and had wild eyes – like an animal trapped in a cage. His voice was raspy and had a resonance to it that was deep and dark. He was much scarier than Johnny.

"I said, who the hell threw that apple at my car," he repeated, getting very loud and sounding angrier by the second.

As per our plan, we all stayed silent – perched in our safe-haven up in the tree. The man was determined to get an answer to his question. He began to climb the second tree, which was the easiest to climb. Samantha and I were both up in that tree. He was much more determined than Johnny – as well as much angrier – and he was quickly getting up the tree toward us. I began to panic, and decided we had better play 'left to right' and get as far away from him as we could. I began to inch my way up higher into the tree, and started to make my way toward the next tree on the right. Sam was quick to follow, and she looked extremely frightened. We were close to getting to the third tree when the man found himself stuck. He had gotten to a tight spot, and he was too large to pass through. Thank God!

"Don't think this is over you little shits, you will pay for hitting my car, mark my words," he yelled as he started his descent. When he was about halfway to the ground, his footing slipped, and he plummeted straight down, landing on his back with a loud "ooompff." Mia began to laugh, despite knowing she shouldn't, and this angered the man even more.

"Oh, so you think this is hilarious, do you? Well, keep on laughing you fucking shits. We will see who is laughing when I find out who you are and where you live. I guarantee, you will not be laughing then!"

With that last rant, he hobbled back to his car, got in and drove down the block. We were all extremely relieved – and afraid to leave the safety of the trees. It was a lucky thing we didn't get down right away because the man circled back around the block, went down the alley, and came back around for another look at the apple bandits! Now we were all scared, even Mia looked a little pale in the face.

"Perhaps that wasn't a good idea after all," Mia said, looking forlorn.

"You can say that again," Jessi replied. "He said he was going to find out where we live – he is going to tell our parents!"

We stayed up in the trees for what seemed like eternity, until we heard a voice from down below say, "I don't think you kids should throw any more of my crabapples at cars."

It was Mrs. Maloney. She had seen the whole thing go down.

"We are sorry Mrs. Maloney," I volunteered, "We won't throw apples at cars anymore, we promise!"

"Well, OK then lovees, I think it is a good idea if you all got home now, before that man comes back looking for you again."

As Mrs. Maloney made her way back to her house, we got down from the trees. We were all pretty shocked. How could we not have foreseen that *someone* would be mad that we hit their car with an apple? After all, Johnny was pretty mad. We all vowed never to throw apples at any moving vehicles again – even Johnny's car – because that was a close call and none of us liked close calls.

Before walking home, we all pinky swore that we wouldn't tell anyone what had happened at Starbort and Port that day. We knew if our parents found out, we would be in terrible, terrible trouble. We were all in trouble on a regular basis as it was, we didn't need that kind of heat. We agreed to meet back at Starbort and Port the next morning after breakfast to think of something new to do. We felt relieved and safe and knew our friends would never tell on us. However, what we didn't know was that someone else had seen us throwing apple bombs, and he didn't pinky swear not to tell.

Chapter 8

"It was Johnny, wasn't it Mom," Ryan asked with anxiousness in his voice. "He told on you, and he got you all in trouble, didn't he?"

"It wasn't Johnny, you twit, it was Mom's cousin,Kyle, he was always watching them and couldn't wait to tell on them" Mark retorted, with almost a hint of pride in his voice. I guess he had been listening after all.

"You are right Mark, he was the one who busted us all! He told my Aunt, who told my Mom, who called Mia's Mom. In one fell-swoop all three of us were all busted. Each of us was grounded to the house for a week. No playing, no phone calls, no nothing. I had the added bonus as the 'thrower' of the apple of having extra chores."

"What about Jessi, Sam and Stephanie?" Mark asked.

Surprised and thrilled that he was finally taking an interest in my story, I decided to continue. The hardest part was still to be revealed, and I was so grateful that he was listening to me.

"Well, Jessi's brother had already ratted us out to her parents. Jessi was grounded for a week and she had to wash Johnny's car. This seemed to appease him, at least for a while," I reported. "Stephanie and Sam escaped the rumor mill. Their Mom wasn't home, and their cousin Angie was babysitting them. When my Mom tried calling there, she got Angie and decided it better to wait to tell Mrs. Ferris, so she said she would call back. Apparently, she forgot, because Stephanie and Samantha were never grounded."

"Lucky for them," Mark added.

"Well, no Mark. It wasn't lucky for them. Sometimes getting into trouble is a good thing. Sometimes a lesson learned can save future heartache later. Imagine what would have happened if we had really done some damage. What if we had hurt someone," I responded.

"Mom, why are you upset?" Ryan asked, obviously worried.

"She is upset because she is worried about me," Mark added. "She is worried that I won't learn and will do bad things like she did. She is afraid that I am a bad kid like she was."

While this was a small part of it, that was not at all why I was upset. Yes, I was worried about my son – both of my sons – and I hoped that my lesson would not fall on deaf ears. Yes, I thought I wasn't a very well-behaved child – neither was my son – but that was just one characteristic of me, and of him.

"I am upset because being grounded was one of the best things that ever happened to me. My Mom and Dad grounded me when I got into trouble – they were trying to teach me what was right and what was wrong. While I was mad and upset at the time, I understand now how hard it was for them to deal with me and my behavior. Being grounded – punished in general – was my saving grace."

"Were you punished a lot Mom?" Ryan asked me.

"Actually, yes I was. It seemed I was always getting into trouble – despite my parents' best attempt to teach me otherwise. In fact, the very next day after the apple bombing escapade I was into trouble again."

"How did you get into trouble if you were grounded?" Mark asked me.

"I didn't listen to my Mom and Dad. In fact, I was being extremely disrespectful to them. In hindsight I can see just how my actions must have been totally heartbreaking for them," I responded as I began to recall those long, two weeks of grounding.

The morning after our apple throwing escapades, I
was in my room pouting. Pouting and thinking about
how totally unfair this punishment was. I was angry
that my stupid cousin ratted us out again! I was mad
that I was going to have to wash dishes and fold
laundry. Most of all, I was mad that on this gorgeous,
sunny day, I was going to be stuck in my house! Dumb
ass cousin!

I didn't have to pout very long before I heard a
tapping at my window. My bedroom was on the
ground floor – easy for my ungrounded friends to come
rapping at my window. I looked out and there stood
Steph and Sam.

"Hey Kayla, your Mom told us you were grounded,"
they reported.

"Yeah, my stupid cousin ratted me out. Now I am
stuck here incommunicado for a stinken' week. How
did you guys not get into trouble?"

"My Mom wasn't home last night. Our cousin,
Angie, answered the phone when your Mom called. I
guess she forgot to call back!"

The truth was, Stephanie and Samantha's Mom
wouldn't have grounded them anyway. She was very
lax when it came to punishments. More of that

divorced parents' incentive program I mentioned earlier.

"So, can you sneak out?" they asked me, looking hopeful.

"Hmmmm, I am not sure. My Mom has been bringing me laundry to fold. I will have to wait a while. Come back in about an hour and I will see if I can get out."

I knew to sneak out I would have to keep my Mom out of my room. To keep my Mom out of my room, I would have to find a good excuse. I decided to play the sick card. I went downstairs to the laundry room and planted the seed.

"Mom, my stomach hurts, and I have a headache," I moaned.

"Hmmm, let me feel you. You don't feel warm. Do you feel nauseous or just like you have to go potty?" she asked.

"I am not sure, I feel kind of dizzy."

"Why don't you go lay down, and I will check on you later," she told me.

Now all I had to do was to pass the 'sleeping' test. I went to my room, drew my blinds and got into my bed.

I relaxed and just tried to look sick. I stayed there, not moving, not talking, not doing anything until she came to check on me. It took almost 45 minutes – which was cutting close to my one-hour deadline with Steph and Sam – but I still had time.

My Mom entered my room, walked over to my bed, listened for noises and then walked back out. I was golden! I knew – or thought I knew – that my sickness bought me at least an hour or two of free play.

I fluffed up some pillows under my covers – the lamest and oldest trick in "Dummies Guide for Fooling Your Parents" – and slipped out my window. Steph and Sam were waiting on the side of my house.

"I have about an hour or two," I announced, feeling cocky. "Let's go see if we can spring Mia!"

Knowing Mia was in the basement meant we could possibly get her out and about as well. Especially since her mother was pregnant and now took these long naps during the afternoons. We snuck down the block and into Mia's backyard. We crouched down on the ground and tapped on her window. In just a few seconds Mia's distorted face appeared behind the block glass basement window.

"Hey, can you sneak out?" we whispered.

"Yeah, my Mom has a headache, I will be out in a minute, meet me behind the garage."

We went to the back of the garage and waited. And waited. And waited. My time was wasting away fast, I sure hoped Mia showed up soon. As if she had read my mind, she popped around the side of the garage.

"Hey guys! How did you all get out?" she asked, out of breath.

"I snuck out and Steph and Sam didn't get into trouble," I responded.

We knew we only had a little bit of time, so we decided to go to Starbort and Port and climb trees. We played 'left to right' and 'cowgirl ranch.' Samantha loved to play ranch, she said when she grew up she was going to have tons of horses and live on a ranch. Her future plans were very specific, she was going to marry a man named Ralph who was a businessman and who owned a horse ranch. She was going to have 3 children, twin boys and a girl. She was going to be a stay at home Mom, and bake cookies and cook and be a great wife. She was going to live a happy life and never, ever get divorced.

Anyway, the third tree from the left had the best, low branches for riding. Mia was the ranch owner and

Steph, Sam and I were the riders. We had a ball taking thin sticks and whipping our horses to ride faster. It was all fun and games until something happened.

In the middle of playing, one of the branches broke with a loud "SNAAAAAAP" and Samantha fell quickly down to the ground. She started crying immediately. We all assumed she was just scared, as the branches were not too far from the ground, but she was really wailing. *Really* wailing loudly!

The rest of us ran to her and assessed the damage. Her arm was turning blue and black already – we knew she wasn't faking.

"I fell right on my elbow," Sam cried. "It hurts really bad!"

There was no time to worry about being in trouble, we had to get Sam home to her Mom. We walked her down the street as she whimpered and cried – obviously in pain. As we walked past my cousin's house, we saw the curtains part and Matt looked out at us, obviously curious as well as angry we had not come to get him. I knew my cover was blown.

When we got Samantha home and in the house, her Mom took one look at her and said, "it is off the ER for you little missy."

After we told her what had happened, Stephanie and Samantha got into their car and sped off. I felt bad for Sam. We were surely not having very good luck right now. As I looked across the street, I saw my Mom looking out the front window – a phone up to her ear – and knew that I was in big, big trouble now. My cousin's big mouth had broken the sound barrier! Mia also knew that she was busted – and she headed back toward her house with a slow, mournful step.

When I got home my Mom was furious! I told her what happened to Samantha, and her response was one I hadn't expected. She looked at me, took my head in her hands and said, "Samantha wouldn't have been hurt if you hadn't snuck out to go down to your trees, now would she?"

I hadn't thought about that. Now I felt even worse – as well as guilty. I was informed that my one week of grounding had magically multiplied into two weeks. I was also told if I ever pulled a stunt like sneaking out of the house and lying about being sick that I would regret it. I believed her. I wish I could say that I never snuck out again – but I did. Despite this lesson, I did sneak out again. I was actually proud that I could fool my parents enough to sneak out. I didn't learn that lesson. Another example of how I thought my parents were just being unreasonable and mean, not that they actually may have a reason for the things that they did. I wish more than anything that I had learned that lesson the first time.

Later that night Mia was allowed to call me to say that she, too, was grounded for two weeks. Her Mom was very upset, mainly because Mia's little escapade turned her headache into a migraine. My Mom and Mia's Mom collaborated on our punishments – knowing if one was out and about the risk of an escape plan would be more imminent. Therefore, keeping us both in punishment was the best option.

Mrs. Ferris also called to report that Samantha's elbow was broken. She was in a cast from her shoulder to her wrist which she would have to wear for the rest of the summer. My Mom informed her that I was grounded, and Mrs. Ferris said she would make sure her girls didn't come tapping on my window.

For the next week and a half, life was pretty boring. My Mom let me into our backyard every once and a while, if she was outside. She said it was so I didn't 'wilt.' Other than that, my face didn't see the light of day for those two weeks. I did more loads of laundry than I ever wanted to, cleaned, dusted and even helped my Mom make price tags for a garage sale she was having on Friday. I was a servant in my own home. I guess I deserved it.

On the day of our garage sale, I had been grounded for 12, long, endless days. I would have done anything to get out of my room. Our driveway and garage were loaded full of items to sell. She was selling all my old stuffed animals, clothes, kitchen stuff, toys and baby items. It was a world-class rummage fest. My Aunt and cousins came to help, and Mia's Mom came to look at baby items. Jessi came down too – as well as Stephanie and Samantha and their Mom - so it wasn't like I was grounded any longer. This was the first time I had seen Samantha up close after her fall – and seeing her made me very sad. Her cast was turning a dingy gray already, and her sister had adorned it with doodle. She asked me if I wanted to sign it too, which I did. I told her I was sorry, and she looked at me like I was crazy. Clearly, she didn't think her injury was my fault. I was very glad for that.

The garage sale had a ton of people – including the Delaneys. When Mrs. Delaney and Star started walking up the driveway our parents immediately started whispering, "Wow, they are out during the day," and "Her daughter looks like she never bathes!"

Mrs. Delaney was looking at stuffed animals for Star, and she kept using words like 'groovy' and 'righteous' when she picked up and looked at items. She ended up spending quite a bit of money, and when she paid she took her money from her bra. "God's natural purse," she said, as my Mom just took the money and smiled. With a quick wave and a "Peace and love" Mrs. Delaney and Star were gone.

"They are odd people," Mia's Mom said.

"Yes, that poor girl. I don't think she knows how to speak," my Mom responded.

"They smell like cardamom or something," Mrs. Ferris said.

"I think that is incense that you smell," my Aunt chimed in.

The Delanyes were not the strangest people to come to my Mom's sale. At the end of the day, before my Mom closed down, a man came wandering up our driveway. He was weaving as he walked, and looked sort of sickly. My Mom whispered to my Aunt that he looked 'stoned' – whatever what meant. He picked up things, wobbled around, almost fell over my old Sit-N-Spin and just generally looked strange.

We were sitting at a small table drinking the lemonade I had decided to try and sell and the man stopped and stared at us. I mean he *stared* at us hard. "What pretty girls you all are," he said, in an almost creepy voice. "Yes, *very* pretty girls indeed."

Sensing that something was not right with him, my Mom came over and informed him that we were closing up. He snapped out of his trance, apologized for keeping us, turned and left. He was a very odd man and he gave me the creeps. Even more so when he turned and look back at us. Gave me shivers up my spine.

 "Mom says when men look at you like that they are undressing you with their eyes," Mia said.

"Ewwww, that is gross!" Stephanie protested.

It was gross. Just thinking about it creeps me out. The image of that man's stare still haunts me today. I think if anyone had looked at my kids that way, I would knock them out!

With the garage sale over my friends all went home and I was once again left in solitude to serve out the rest of my sentence. Only two more days – I was really hoping I could get time off for good behavior. I made it through the first day without a hitch – but I was getting impatient. Me plus impatience always equaled trouble!

My mother had decided to allow me to use the phone on my last day of punishment – a most welcome advantage. I called Mia, but she wasn't home. I wonder where SHE got the privilege of going? I called over to Steph and Sam's and Steph answered the phone.

"Man Kayla, it sucks that you are still grounded. I got a new hop-n-skip and I really wanted to have a contest with you," Steph announced.

"What the heck is a hop-n-skip," I inquired, having no idea.

"It's awesome! You put your one foot in this loop thing then swing it around and hop over it. There is a counter thing-a-ma-do too that tells you how many times you have skipped. I thought we could have a contest and see who could do it most!"

I was bummed. New toys were definitely my forte. I had one, stinken' day of grounding left. I wondered if my Mom would let me go out just one day early. I thought about it for all of a milli-second and decided that I could get myself out – one way or another.

"Hey Steph, I bet I can get out for a while. My Mom has been really cool lately and I think I can persuade her to let me out on early release. How about I meet you at Starbort and Port in a half hour?"

"Cool Kayla. I'll see ya down there," she replied in a most cheery sing-song way.

I figured if Mom wouldn't let me out – or if I couldn't sneak out – the worst that would happen is Steph would have to skip and hop alone, no big whoop!

I went to find my Mom, who was making brownies in the kitchen.

"Hey Mom, do you think I could got out, just for a little bit? I want to see Steph's new toy and . . . "

"Now Kayla," my Mom interrupted, giving me that *are you serious* look, "you know you have to be grounded until tomorrow. One more day won't kill you."

"FINE!" I retorted, "one, more, SUCKY day in this house!"

I stormed off back to my room, not at all surprised. I thought for a moment about sneaking out, but knew my Mom would come and check on me, now that I had alerted her to my plans to play. I decided against it, and just stayed in my room. Sometimes being good really sucked. I guess I could wait one more day to see this magical hop-n-jump thing.

Chapter 9

Later that afternoon, the phone rang. Just a normal sound – a phone ringing – but this time the ring sounded . . . deeper, louder, different. Knowing that I was *still* grounded, I didn't even attempt to answer it, 'cause I was sick of talking on the phone. However, holding on to the glimpse of hope that one of my friends would convince my Mom to let me out, I opened my door to eavesdrop.

"Hi Tracy. - No, I haven't seen Samantha today. No, Kayla is still grounded, she is in her room.   Yes, yes, I am sure she is in there, she had better be anyway………. No, she asked if she could go out, I said 'no' and she has been here ever since…… Well, when did she leave?………… OK, if I see her, I will let you know. Ok, bye now."

"Kayla, can you come here for a moment," my Mom yelled to me.

"Yeah Mom."

"You haven't snuck out your window today, or let anyone in your room, have you?"

My Mom knew that with me it was better to ask than assume. On this particular day, however, I had chosen the higher road and was actually telling the truth.

"No Mom, I have been folding laundry and cleaning my room, like I have been every sucky day for the last two sucky weeks, why?"

"Well, Mrs. Ferris said she can't find Sam. Apparently, Stephanie wasn't feeling so well this afternoon, so she sent Sam down to those trees where you guys play to relay that message to *you*. She *thought* you were meeting Stephanie down there. Mrs. Ferris said she has been gone for 3 hours and hasn't checked back in."

"Did she call Mia's house to see if she was there?"

"I guess she has looked all over – even at Mr. Bartlett and Mr. Jonas' house. She isn't anywhere on the block."

"I am sure she is around somewhere. Did you check with Mrs. Maloney?" I offered.

"Mrs. Ferris says she has checked everywhere. She is going to go and search the neighborhood. I am sure she is just somewhere she shouldn't be – like Dairy Queen."

My Mom knew that we kids were always riding to the local Dairy Queen. Around the corner from our play spot was a line of apartment buildings. If we rode our bikes behind them, we would end up at Dairy Queen.

None of us was allowed to go there alone – or without asking – but we had been known, on occasion, to sneak down there. Sam loved dilly bars – but I wasn't sure she would go there alone. She was a pretty timid girl – at least compared to the rest of us. I guess it was more that I was hoping that was where she was.

Remembering that day – that phone call – brought back all kinds of emotions. I will never forget that day - July 20, 1983 - I was 12 years old. I was extremely naïve. I never thought that anything bad had happened to Sam. I assumed, as did the rest of our gang, that she was just playing somewhere. We had done a lot of stupid things, but nothing *really* bad ever happened to us. We were definitely blessed with good luck amongst our bad judgment. It was inevitable that our luck would eventually shift.

Remembering my nonchalant attitude about Sam was evoking intense emotion. The tears started running freely from my eyes. I tried hard not to cry in front of my boys. Somehow, I thought my job as their Mom was to be strong and not to get overly emotional in front of them. Thinking about it I wondered why I thought this was a good thing. We are all tied together by emotions. It is our ability to connect to others based on likes or dislikes, hate, fear, love – why would I ever hide any emotions, especially one as powerful as sadness or regret. So, the tears fell and the sadness crept in.

"Mommy, why are you crying?" Ryan asked, looking upset.

"Ry, I am crying because I should. I am here with you and your brother trying to connect with you, to reveal something to you that is really important. I am afraid for you, and for Mark. I am afraid because the world is truly full of bad people; bad people who do bad things. I am praying that neither of you will ever meet any truly bad people in your lives."

Bad people. I have met and faced some really bad people. Didn't always know it at the time, but they were very, very bad people. I shudder to think of all the decisions that I have made that have jeopardized my safety. The impulsivity. The defiance. Ignoring the wise words of my parents, or even that little internal voice that whispered, *do you really want to do that*?

Sometimes God or whomever is out there in the universe, sends you a message to not do something, to stay away from a person or place, or to turn left instead of right, to not go to the party, or not to drink another drink. That intuitive voice is the whisper of God. We need to listen to that voice – learn to hear it instead of blocking it. Sometimes God chooses to save you – for whatever reason – and perhaps sacrifice another. This is the way the world works. God saved me - and sometimes, I wonder why.

Chapter 10

A few hours after Mrs. Ferris had called, the phone started ringing off the hook. The neighborhood rumor mill had been kicked into overdrive. Code Red! Everyone wanted to know where Sam was, and the assumptions were already starting. My Mom was careful to not talk too loudly, but I could still hear the worried tone in her voice. The continuous answers of, "I don't know" and "I am sure she is fine" were getting less and less convincing with every phone call. Around ten o'clock in the evening there was a knock at our door. I had been told to go to sleep, but I was worried about Sam and I was not about to drift into dreamland when one of our gang was missing.

I heard a man's voice speaking to my father – a voice I had not heard before – and soon the voices got louder. Sitting in the kitchen, which was right off my room, I could hear the conversation perfectly. Apparently, he was a police officer who was interviewing all the people in the neighborhood in an effort to find Sam. It didn't take long for the officer to suggest he speak to me, as I was the person who Sam was supposed to meet down at the corner.

"Kayla honey, can you come here please?" my Dad asked, knowing I was up and listening at my door.

When I got into the kitchen, the rather young officer introduced himself, holding his hand out formally.

"Hi Kayla, my name is Officer Montgomery, I am going to help to find your friend Sam."

I returned the introduction, then asked how I could help.

"Kayla, it is very important that you tell me the absolute truth to all the questions I will ask you, do you understand?" he asked, with a very calm demeanor.

"I understand," I answered, gulping down a bit of fear and panic. Here was a police officer in my house, talking to me. I had not been the best friend to Sam lately, as it was my fault she had broken her arm in the first place. I was feeling immensely guilty – and very panicked – but I was willing to be in trouble for the rest of my life if it would help Sam.

Officer Montgomery asked me about today, when I told Stephanie to meet me down at the corner. I told him that I was planning on going, but my Mom had said I couldn't go out. I had actually decided not to risk more grounding and stayed in, but had forgotten to call and tell Steph. I explained how we met at the trees at the end of the block, how we all played there, and how it was special to all of us.

"Kayla, your Mom and Mrs. Ferris have told me that you frequently sneak out when you are grounded, is that correct," he asked, looking at me from over the top of his little notebook.

"Yes sir, that is true. Today I didn't sneak out though, 'cause my Mom would have known if I did," I answered honestly.

"Kayla, it is very important that we know exactly when Sam was down at the corner and if anyone was with her. If you did go out, and you did see Sam, it is very important that you tell us," he probed again.

My Mom chimed in as well, "Kayla honey, if you snuck out, I won't be mad at you, and I will not ground you for it. We just really need to know if you did so we can find Sam."

"I didn't sneak out. I know I have lied about this before, but I didn't today! I swear! I pinky swear! I swear to *God*. I really am telling the truth," I answered, the tears started to flow from my eyes. I could no longer hide the guilt.

"Kayla, we believe you honey. Now, if you can just tell us if Sam came by your window before she headed down to the corner, or if you had any contact with her after you decided not to meet Stephanie," Officer Montgomery probed.

"I didn't see her at all. The last time I saw her was Friday at the garage sale my Mom had," I answered.

Thinking of the last time I had seen my friend. What if that was the last time I ever saw Sam. Where in the world can she be? Sam would never be gone at night alone, she was too afraid of ghosts and zombies and monsters. This was not like her. Not like her at all.

The officer said he had all he needed from me for the moment. He wrote a few things in his notebook, then walked to the front door.

"Officer Montgomery," I stopped him at the door, "are you going to find Sam?"

"Kayla, we are going to try our best. We have all our best officers out looking right now. All your neighbors are looking for her. We will do our best to find her, I promise," he said, with a self-confident air that made me feel slightly more secure.

After Officer Montgomery left, my Mom told me to get some sleep. My father was going out with his flashlight with Mia's Dad and my Uncle to look in the train fields that ran behind our house. We were never supposed to play in those fields because of old, rusty train spikes or the possibility of snakes. Sam was petrified of the train yards, so I doubt she would have gone back there. I suppose it was good to look everywhere though. I was sure she was so scared now, and I really just wanted her to come home.

My Mom, Mia's Mom and my Aunt sat at the table, talking nervously. My Mom had gotten the bottle of dark, brown liquid that she kept above the refrigerator. They were all adding it into their coffee cups, but I did not smell coffee.

"I'll bet it was her bastard ex, he probably took her so he can get even for her divorcing him," my Aunt suggested.

"No, he was a mean son-of-a-bitch, but I doubt he would take one of his daughters," Mia's Mom chimed in. "Not to mention, I am sure the cops have checked him out already."

"If I had to choose," my Mom offered, "I would pray it was her Dad, because at least then she would be safe. The alternative makes me sick to my stomach. I can't even imagine if one of my kids was missing!"

"Why was she down there anyway, alone, without Stephanie?" my Aunt questioned.

"She was going there to tell Kayla that Stephanie wasn't coming. Kayla wasn't there because I wouldn't let her out of her grounding," my Mom informed them.

"Well, Georgia, I am sure you are grateful that Kayla listened, or she could have been taken too!"

Taken?

This was the first time I had heard that Sam was taken. Taken by whom? Taken where? Why would someone take Sam? So, she wasn't just hiding somewhere, they thought she had been taken! I pushed my face into my pillow to muffle the sound of my sobs. Someone may have taken my friend, and it was all my fault.

That was the longest night of my life. I remember that I did not sleep that entire night. I could hear one voice after another calling out, "Samaaannnthaaaa!" in the darkness of the night. And I never heard her answer the call.

Chapter 11

"Mommy, did someone take your friend Sam," Ryan asked me, looking very sad.

"Yes honey, someone did take her," I answered him, taking his little head in my hands.

"Did she come home Mom," Mark asked, "I mean, it was just her Dad who took her right, to get back at Sam's Mom? You hear about that all the time, parents snatching their kids to get back at another parent. What is that thing they do, Amber alerts? I am sure they just put out one of those and she came home, right Mom?"

Unfortunately, back in 1983 there was no Amber Alert. In 1983 there were very few proactive methods in place to help locate a child who was missing, or God forbid, abducted. What there was, however, were family and friends. When Sam went missing — technically she was not deemed abducted for 24 hours - the whole neighborhood came together to find her. Everyone on the block — and I mean *everyone* — trudged through the train fields, knocked on doors for miles around, posted flyers with her picture, asked people in grocery stores. Everyone came together as a cohesive unit to try and find Sam.

Even Mr. Jonas, who was normally uninterested in anything that concerned us neighborhood kids, brought flyers to the city with him, asking people on the train if they had heard anything about Sam. He had told my father that "The first 48 hours are the most critical, and it was of importance to make it known that Sam was missing and see if anyone saw anything." He often explained things to other neighbors when it came to deciphering all the "police talk." My opinion of Mr. Jonas as an uncaring person truly changed after these events.

Pastor Rider opened up his church as a sort of headquarters for all the searchers. His parishioners came and provided food for the policeman – and eventually the FBI agents – as well as offered prayers for everyone involved. Many people in our neighborhood started to come to his prayer services. We all lit candles and said prayers that Sam would come home safe and sound. I didn't exactly understand the significance of lighting little candles, but I thought it was oddly calming. Almost like the little lights amongst the darkness were hundreds of fireflies.

Pastor Rider worked tirelessly, sleeping in the church sanctuary, and he was a constant reminder that without faith there is nothing but despair. We had faith. We all had a lot of faith in the beginning.

However, as the minutes and hours ticked by – our faith started to dwindle. As the days started passing, faith was nowhere to be found. It changed us all.

Chapter 12

By the third day with no sign of Sam, the FBI was called in to assist. They set up in the church next door and there were hundreds of people going in and out of that church. FBI agents, volunteers to answer the phones for all the "have you seen Samantha Ferris" tips, people from the block, searchers, specialists on hair and fiber, the dog handlers. I was so curious as to what was going on over there. I kept my ears peeled to figure out what and who everyone was. I overheard my Mom telling Mia's Mom that the dogs were going to sniff some of Sam's clothing and try to find a scent. Apparently, these dogs could detect the scent of her for miles around. With a large, open train field behind our houses the dogs could search faster than humans. I found that fascinating! On the evening of the third day I got a close-up look inside the "command" center when I was requested for questioning.

My father walked me over and I was holding his hand so tightly I thought it would bruise him! Inside the church sanctuary were these large boards with pictures of Sam, our block from every imaginable angle, Starbort and Port, everyone's cars, license plates, all the houses on the block with addresses and names, and a head shot of almost every neighbor on our block. There were other boards with writing under bold

headlines: "Suspects"; "Motives"; "Witnesses."
Familiar names and names I had never seen were
scribbled on these boards. I felt very, very
overwhelmed and scared looking at it all. It made me
feel sort of faint, so I grabbed my father's hand more
tightly.

"Hello there Mr. Harrison, thank you for bringing
Kayla over, I am Special Agent Griffin," said an older
man as he held out his hand to my father.

"Kayla," my father said gently, "Mr. Griffin works for
the FBI. He is a special agent who is going to try really
hard to find what happened to Samantha. He needs to
ask you some questions and I need you to always
answer him honestly no matter what. Do you
understand?"

"Yes, Dad."

"Hello there Kayla," Mr. Griffin extended his hand to
me, "Can we go over here and sit so I can ask you some
questions that may help to find Sam?"

I sat down on the nearest pew, scooching over to give
Mr. Griffin some space. My father sat a pew up, within
ear shot, and stared at all the white boards at the front
of the church. I knew that this had softened him, that

my Dad was less harsh after this, more loving and gentle. More thankful for his family being in-tact.

"Kayla, I have read the transcript of your previous interview with Officer Montgomery. It says that you planned to meet Stephanie at the corner lot but that you did not go, is that still your statement today?"

"Yesss.....Ssssir."

"OK. So, then you did not see Samantha at all the day that she went missing?"

"Yes, Sir. I mean, no Sir. I mean, I did not see Sam that day."

"Kayla, this next question is very important. We know that you and your friends spent a lot of time down there at the corner. We know that you would play on the trees down there. We know that Samantha fell from the tree branch and broke her elbow not too long ago, is that correct?"

Where was he going with this? Was I going to be arrested for sneaking out of the house and making my friend break her arm? I answered, "Yeesss, Sir. She fell off while we were playing Dude Ranch and broke her elbow. It is why I was grounded. I had snuck out that day," lowering my head in shame as the tears rolled down my cheek.

"Kayla, we also know that you have had a few "incidents" where you and your friends threw some crabapples at cars as they drove around the corner, is that correct?" he asked with a curious intonation.

"Yeeess. We accidentally hit one of my friend's brother's cars and thought it was funny....but we know it is not funny NOW," I hurriedly responded, trying to show him we knew it was wrong.

"It is OK Kayla. John told us all about that. I am more interested in knowing if you hit any other cars?"

"Yeeees. Actually. I hit a man's car and he was really angry. I had never seen someone so angry! He ran after us and swore at us and called us names!"

"OK, can you tell me more about this," he asked, flipping to a new page in his book.

I described that day's events from the terms of our "game," to the car that I had hit with the apple.

"Kayla, can you remember what color his car was and what it looked like?"

I described the bright blue sports car. Mr. Griffin showed me pictures of styles of cars and it was determined to be a Corvette. He even had color swatches to show me so I could find the exact blue of the car. As soon as I had identified the car, Mr. Griffin called an officer over and told him to do a search for registered vehicles of this make and model by requisitioning the DMV records. I had no idea what any of this meant....DMV...requisition...all these terms had my head spinning!

"Kayla, this is VERY important. I need you to describe to me in as much detail as possible what this man looks like."

It had been quite a while ago, but I would never forget that face and those wild, deep green eyes. I told Mr. Griffin everything that I could remember, which was actually quite a lot. He then called a man over who had a sketch pad and I told him what I remembered. When I was done describing him, the artist turned to show me his drawing and there was a good image of the man I had angered with my apple throwing.

I stared back at this image. This white man with a thin face, scar on upper right cheek under the eye. Dark, brown hair that was thick and almost curly. Deep, dark, green eyes. Crooked teeth and one missing on the top. The sight made me get chills it was so accurate.

"This is a great start, Kayla, you did very well," Agent Griffin praised me.

"Um, why did I need to describe him?" I asked.

"Kayla, when someone goes missing, especially a child, it is important to think of anyone and everyone who could have possibly had motive to take that child. Do you know what "motive" is?" he asked.

"Um, a reason to do something."

"Exactly. So, when we started to investigate what happened to Sam, we asked everyone on this block if they thought there was anyone who could have had any involvement or reason to take or hurt Sam."

"How did you know about our game?" I asked him.

"Mrs. Maloney was questioned regarding seeing Samantha. I asked her the same things I asked every other person on this block about motives and she remembered the day this man had chased you all up the trees. She did not get a good enough view of him to describe him, other than his hair color and height, so I wanted to confirm with you."

"Ooooooh...."

"Now, Kayla this is also a very important question. Do you remember your Mom's garage sale?"

"Yes. It was just last Friday."

"Do you remember a man who came at the end and was staggering around, sort of looking at all of you?"

"Oh yeah, he was creeeeepy!" I responded, remembering the way he "undressed us with his eyes."

Mr. Griffin pulled a paper from a folder and presented it to me, "Does this look like the man at the garage sale?" he asked.

I looked at the picture and sure enough it looked just like the man from the sale.

"Yes! That is him! How did you get his picture?"

"Your Mother and neighbors described him, which was enough to find out who he is and where he lives. Now, have you seen him around your block either before or after the sale?"

"No, I have never seen him before and I have not been out of the house much since the sale."

"OK Kayla. You did very, very well. I want to thank you for all your honest answers and help. I want to assure you that we will do everything possible to find your friend!"

I couldn't help it. I jumped up and hugged him. I believed that he would really, truly do everything he could to find Samantha. I was grateful to him and I was happy to have helped in any way I could. The guilt was killing me as it was.

Chapter 13

"OK, so I am sure they just put those sketches into the computer system and found out who these guys were by their fingerprints or mugshot and one of them took Sam, right Mom?" Mark asked me with honest enthusiasm.

Again, Mark did not understand that in 1983 there was not facial recognition software. There were barely fingerprint databases, and what they did have was slow and not very well connected. In fact, there were not even household computers, not to mention the internet. Sure, the police and FBI had rudimentary computer systems, but they were not like they are today. He takes for granted the world he lives in with television he can pause or skip the commercials on, Wi-Fi, I-phones, instant access to everything. He watches shows like *CSI* and *Law and Order* and sees how seemingly simple it is to locate someone via fingerprints, hair, fibers, blood. He sees the Amber Alerts pop up on his cellphone, watches the reports on the news when parents abduct their own children, and assumes that it was the same when I was a kid. It wasn't.

What he does not understand and can't even fathom is that *my* world, my youth, was not so technologically advanced. It was painstakingly rudimentary. It was overall a simple time in all ways. Playing, for us kids, involved riding bikes, climbing trees, making forts and being outside. Not like his existence of motorized scooters and sitting on the steps and texting the person sitting next to you instead of talking, and, of course, video games.

Sure, the advancements of the day are wonderful and I wish they had those same advantages when Sam was missing. However, the disadvantage is that the children of today have no idea what it was like before they were born. I suppose this is the cross to bear of any parent. I mean, my Mom told me she had to "walk to school in a foot of snow, uphill both ways" when she pointed out how lucky I was to have a bus to take. Or, remarked how lucky I was to have a phone to call my friends on, a pool in my backyard, a bike with more than one speed. Yeah, the world advances and with each generation we take these things for granted.

What I tried to explain to Mark is that in his world there are so many ways to track a criminal but in 1983, it was all done the "old-fashioned" way. It was posters and flyers and gossip. It was door-to-door searches and regular folks outside with flashlights calling her name. It was a community effort where everyone came together for one greater cause: to find Samantha.

"No, Mark. Times were different then. We had to circulate those flyers and literally go door-to-door asking if anyone had seen those men."

"Did you find them, Mom?" Ry asked.

"That, Ry, is not a simple answer."

After my interrogation with Mr. Griffin I was sure the man who took Sam would be the creepy, garage sale man. I was confident that Sam would be home in a day or two. I was wrong. Days passed and no Sam. They did find the man from the garage sale. He lived a few blocks away and was, apparently, a raging alcoholic. They found him the same day the sketch was distributed. The police checked his house, car, garage and found absolutely no sign of Samantha.

I heard my Mom and Mia's Mom talking and they were saying how they would look for her hair and clothing at his house. That they had special lights that would show blood stains.

BLOOD STAINS!

It had not occurred to me until that moment that Samantha could actually be *dead*. That the man who took her would do her harm. That she really, truly may never be coming back. That I may never play with my friend again. That something bad, horrible, unimaginable had happened to her. That it could be *me* who is missing, or worse, dead!

My stomach flopped and I threw up all over!

The same day they found the garage sale man the FBI agents were doing a very thorough search of the trees at Starbort and Port. They had roped off the entire lot with yellow "POLICE LINE" tapes that we were not allowed to go past. They also had blocked off traffic to our block from the main road. Every car that attempted to go down our street was stopped by a police officer. If you lived on our block you had a special sticker on your car indicating that you were allowed to be here. The irony was that when I read George Orwell's 1984 in Junior High school I thought to myself, *no, that was 1983*!

It was a very sad time. None of us kids were allowed to go anywhere without an escort. If I were to go to Mia's house, I had to have a parent walk me down or stand on the sidewalk as I walked from my house to hers. It felt scary and unnatural. Our little fun-loving haven of childhood innocence was now shattered as we lived in total fear and anxiety. My friends and I felt even less safe, despite the constant circulation of police personnel. Rumors and theories continued to circulate. Our parents were constantly whispering *"Have you heard..."* and *"I think it was..."* and *"No, I didn't hear that.*" If we kids listened carefully we could get most of the scoop.

Mia, Jessi, Matt and I did not know what to do. There were so many people on our little block and we were constantly told that "This is not a place for children" and to "go make another flyer." Personally, we were all sick to death of making fucking flyers. We wanted to see our friend. We all had our theories on what happened to Sam and when she would come home. Our theories always ended with Sam coming home – happy, untouched, unaware that we were all missing her. Our parent's theories were not so "happily ever after" and usually involved funeral services.

When the garage sale guy was cleared, Jessi was sure that it was Mr. Ferris. We had all seen him blow up at Mrs. Ferris too many times and heard the words, "You'll be sorry," coming from his evil, yelling mouth! Jessi was sure that he had a plan to take Sam and then make Mrs. Ferris so grief stricken that she could no longer function. As it turned out, Mr. Ferris had an alibi – which is apparently a person who could vouch for your whereabouts when a certain event took place. My father informed my uncle that Mr. Ferris' alibi was "23, blonde, big busted and slutty." I wondered if his alibi was also the reason Mrs. Ferris hated him so much? In any case, he was with her and they were miles away from our block. Mr. Ferris was in the clear.

In fact, Mr. Ferris was very, very upset that his daughter was missing. He moved in with Mrs. Ferris and Stephanie to help look for Sam. He was constantly out looking for her – day and night – and whenever anyone asked about her he would break down into a fit of weeping. Not manly weeping either – the eyes-get-red-real-tears-nose-running weeping that one would expect from a child. My Mother said no one could fake that type of emotion. When he and Mrs. Ferris spoke to the police or the news media, he had his arm draped around her shoulder in a very comforting manner. To all of us he was no longer the 'prick' of an ex-husband, he was Sam's Dad and he was a total mess.

Mia had a different idea about what happened to Sam. Sam loved Dairy Queen – absolutely loved it. However, she didn't like to go to Dairy Queen with her sister. Whenever we would all go to Dairy Queen together Sam would order the same thing: a banana split with two helpings of cherries and one of butterscotch. She loved banana splits. Stephanie, however, was a bit more indecisive, even though she loved banana splits too. She always ordered something different, but then wanted the split. This resulted in her eating half of Sam's split AND her own selection. This always pissed Sam off.

Operating on this ideal, Mia suspected that Sam went down to the corner to meet me. When I didn't show up she decided to go to Dairy Queen all by herself and have a banana split. No one would suspect she had gone, 'cause Stephanie would think she was playing with me. She would go to DQ, get her split, eat it ALL herself, then come back home. While at DQ she would see a friend who she knew from school and that friend would ask her to go swimming. She would go, but forget to call home, and spend the night. Mia said she was sure when she realized that no one knew where she was that she would call and it would all be OK. Mia was an optimist at heart. While this theory was a very nice one, Mrs. Ferris assured the police that she had called all of Sam's friends – and Stephanie's – and no one had seen or heard from Sam. Plus, after a day or two that theory evaporated quickly – as did all the other theories anyone had.

Matt, of course, had the most outrageous theory of all. He said that Sam went down to Starbort and Port and I was not there. Mrs. Maloney saw her and invited her to have some cookies and lemonade on the porch. Matt, still thinking that nice, sweet, Mrs. Maloney was some sort of evil scientist, said she took Sam to the barn and embalmed her in plaster. Then she covered her with a sheet and left her in the barn with all the other 'solid ghosts' she had piled in there. As outrageous as this theory was, Mrs. Maloney did receive a lot of special attention from the police. As her home was right next to the corner where Sam was last seen, the police took special care in interviewing her. Her barn was opened, and all the sheets were removed from her artwork. Anti-climactic as it was, the sheets simply adorned her sculptures. My Aunt was there for the unveiling and she reported to my Mom that they were mostly sculptures of her late husband in various poses. Fishing, standing, sitting and even reading. It was like a memorial for the love of her life.

Apparently, they were very nicely done. There was nothing other than art supplies and sculptures found in the barn. Also, Mrs. Maloney had been visiting her daughter a few hours away at the time Sam disappeared, so she hadn't seen or heard anything down at the corner. Mrs. Maloney's house was searched thoroughly – as was everyone else's on the block – and nothing of interest was found. She had a basement full of canned goods, lots of old furniture, and pictures of her family. She was extremely upset that Sam was missing, as she did really love all of us.

Stephanie was absolutely inconsolable. She had lost her sister – her *twin* sister – and thought it was all her fault. She refused to talk to us – and I knew she at least partially blamed me. If I hadn't told her that I would meet her down at Starbort and Port, then Sam would never have been there.   Hell, I blamed myself. Whoever or whatever had taken our friend Sam, the fact was, if she was taken from the corner – it was my fault. No one else's just mine.

Chapter 14

"Mom that was not YOUR fault," Mark announced, "you guys played down there all the time. Met each other down there all the time. It could have happened to anyone! In fact, if you had gone it may have been YOU!"

Ahhh, the lightbulb moment for my son!

Exactly what I had been trying to explain to him! But for the grace of GOD it was not me. No. I had narrowly escaped an unknown fate because I chose to listen to my Mom and stay in the house! What if I had snuck out and was making my way down to Starbort and Port and I was the one taken? What if both Sam and I were taken? There is really no way to know what could have happened. All I know is that had I not been cocky, had I not told Stephanie that I would definitely come and meet her, that Sam would not have been there.

That is completely and utterly on me.

Mark was partially right. I could have been me. It could have been Mia, Matt, Jessi. Sure, we all played down there. However, *this* day, this time it was me who was going to sneak out to go down there and play and it was *me* who Sam was going to talk with. No one else. Just *me*.

"Mark, the point is I was a smug little know-it-all, do-what-I-wanted-damn-the-consequences kid. I had snuck out of my house so many times that every one of my friends knew if I said I would get there, I would get there. Stephanie counted on me being there because I said I would. She sent Sam down there because I should have been there. Do you understand?"

"Yeah, I guess."

"Mom, what happened with the police and the trees? Did you ever play there again?" Ry asked.

That was the question of the hour, wasn't it?

The police had those yellow tapes up for a long, long time. At first there were police and FBI agents down there all the time. They had special lights, rakes, shovels, machines and even dogs down there. All of us kids wanted desperately to know what was going on, but none of us felt like we should hang around and watch. We would go to my Aunt's house, which was closest to the corner, and watch out the window or from the front lawn. We watched all the officers putting random things into plastic bags, pouring what appeared to be cement on the ground, sweeping the entire lot with metal detectors. We were curious enough to watch, but scared enough to keep our distance.

111

One day, about a week after Samantha went missing, I was going down to my Aunt's house and I saw Stephanie outside. I wanted to talk to her, to hug her, to say I was sorry. I wanted to ask how she was. I walked across the street and up to her, not saying a word, just giving her a giant hug.

"I am so sorry Steph," I said, starting to cry, "so, so, so sorry."

"Don't be sorry Kayla, it is not your fault," Steph flatly replied. She seemed almost…. emotionless.

"What is happening? Do you know anything? How is your Mom? Have they found any clues?" I rambled all my questions at her.

"Well, they found bits of Sam's arm cast all over the trees and on the ground. My Mom said it looked like she was trying to climb up and was pulled or fell down. They also found bits of her cast on the ground all the way from the trees to almost the street."

"What does that mean?"

"Well, the policeman who was telling my parents said it looked like she fought off whoever was trying to take her and broke some of her cast off along the way."

"Oh Stephanie, I am so, so, so sorry," I said.

Stephanie didn't respond. She just started to weep and
then ran back into her house and slammed the door.
Her mother looked out the window at me and gave me
a weak, sad, wave.

Great. Now I had upset a friend again. I lowered my
head and walked down to my aunt's house.

Matt and I were playing in the basement when we
heard the knock on the door. It was my parents coming
to have coffee with my Aunt and Uncle. We positioned
ourselves by the heat vent and listened, intently, for
any news of Sam.

"I heard that they found a chunk of her hair down
there, like it had been ripped out," my Dad whispered.

"Oh my God!," whispered my Mom and Aunt
simultaneously.

"Yeah, and parts of her cast. Poor, poor, poor girl,"
my Aunt uttered.

My Uncle added, "After all this time, the chances of
finding her are pretty slim and if they do....."

"I know and I hate to think about it," my Aunt said.

"They also have a footprint they are going to plaster
to match to any suspects. Plus, they were trying to

figure out tire prints, but too many cars peel out down there," my Uncle said.

"I know that they found the car that matched the description Kayla had given them," my Mom informed, "but the guy who owns it said it had been stolen 3 months before and they had the police report to confirm it, so that was a total dead end!"

"Crap," I whispered to Matt, "if it was not the garage sale guy, not Mr. Ferris, and they can't find the actual owner of the car, how will they find Sam!"

"The thing is, why would anyone take a little girl? Unless they wanted her for, you know, to *do* things to her...I can't even imagine...it is unfathomable..." my Mom volunteered, sounding like she was crying.

"Georgia, don't think about that. Do not allow yourself to think about that!" my Dad warned.

A sudden feeling of despair filled my heart. I knew, then, that the chances of ever seeing my friend again were slim to none. I realized that even if they found Samantha it would not be a good thing. I knew my friend was probably dead. I knew that none of us would ever be the same.

Chapter 15

The longer Samantha was missing, and the less positive the feelings of finding her were, the more frustrated all of us kids became. Pastor Rider continued to hold vigils for Samantha every Saturday night. At first his prayers were centered around finding Sam, giving her comfort to not be afraid, for the searchers and the police who were working so tirelessly to find her. By the end of the month, those prayers turned to ones of comfort for her parents and friends. By the end of the fourth month, the prayers were less hopeful, and more of asking us to come to grips with the reality. By the fifth month, there was little hope in his prayers, just consolation. One particular prayer he offered was chilling and foretold, in a manner, of what was to come:

"Dear Lord, we come to you again with deep devotion! Thanking you for your goodness, your strength and your undying faith in us. Lord, we acknowledge that in this world there is an evil hidden among us, an evil that runs parallel to our lives, intruding on our sense of peace and security. A wolf in sheep's clothing. The devil in the body of a man. We pray to you, oh Lord, to recognize that evil does exist, temptations do exist, that tragedies we cannot understand do exist but that among all of this so does

hope, love and your everlasting love and light. That,
too, DOES exist! We pray to you, most humbly, that
your light and love shine down on Samantha Ferris now
and forever. That you comfort her. That you fill her
with your love. That you release her from pain and fear.
That you take her in your heavenly arms and love her
and keep her. That Samantha never feel alone within
your heavenly grasp. This is our prayer and wish. Thank
you oh Lord, our Savior! In Jesus' name we pray!
Amen!"

After this prayer the church emptied in silence, with
only the sounds of sniffing and blowing noses.
Samantha's father walked holding Stephanie's hand, his
arm draped firmly around the ex-Mrs. Ferris, all of them
looking years older than they were. My Mom grabbed
my hand so hard I thought it would break, and my Dad
had tears in his eyes. Everyone seemed forlorn and the
tone was no longer hopeful, but one of deep grief and
acceptance.

That night, in bed, I prayed to God. I prayed for
forgiveness for my part in this tragedy. I prayed that
Sam know how much we all loved her. I prayed, still,
that she come home but I also prayed that she not be
hurt or dead. That if she were to never come back that
the person who took her at least was being kind and
nice to her. That she was riding horses somewhere and

laughing. I prayed that my friend was not in pain. I prayed for that because I could not bring myself to imagine the alternative.

A few months later, Matt, Mia, Jessi and I felt depressed. Eight months and still not a clue about Sam. Stephanie never came out of her house, ever. It was like we had lost two friends instead of one. The FBI agents had abandoned their post at the corner, the yellow police tapes tattered and waving in the late, February breeze. The church had gone back to almost normal now, the police moving their headquarters to the police station. People tried to resume normalcy, going to work and continuing on with life. My Mom said that "life goes on" and she was right. Eventually, those of us left behind had to realize that we were still here and try to live our lives.

"What are we supposed to do now?" Matt asked, "I don't want to play at Starbort and Port any more."

"I know, me neither," Mia chimed, "but I don't want to just sit on the steps either."

I was outraged that the police had given up so easily! I felt that 8 months was not long enough to search for a little girl – for *my* friend! I had heard all the statistics about finding her after this amount of time, about how she was likely dead, about how the police could not continue to devote resources every day looking for Sam. I thought it was all bullshit! I did not want to give up! I wanted to DO something.

"The police had to miss something!" I whined.

"Kayla, they searched everywhere – e v e r y where – on this block and for blocks around! They did not miss anything," Mia retorted.

In my head I knew she was right, but in my heart, I felt differently. I needed to do something, to be proactive! I needed to put my head into something positive.

"I think we need to make a memorial for her, you know, like a tombstone type thing," I suggested.

"But she doesn't have a grave, where would we put it?" Matt asked.

"We should put it at Starbort and Port, as a remembrance of our friend and where she was last seen," I said.

"Yeah...we need to do that. What should we make?" Mia asked.

"I will grab some of those pieces of wood from my Dad's workshop and make a cross. Then, we can paint it and put it down there by her favorite tree, you know, the one with the branches that reminded her of horses.....” my voice trailing off in sadness.

“Ok then. We will meet in my garage tomorrow afternoon. I have some leftover paint and we can make it look really pretty,” Mia said.

I ran home as fast as I could and found just the wood pieces I was looking for. I grabbed a hammer and some nails and headed up to my tree house. For some reason, I felt this was a quiet moment and I did not want my Mom asking me what I was up to. I climbed up and was stopped dead in my tracks! On each wall we had all scribbled different doodles. Staring back at me was a horse that Sam had drawn with a stick figure cowgirl riding it. Under it read, “My Dream!” I couldn’t hold it in any longer. I started to weep. Seriously weep. The guilt, the anger, the frustration, the loneliness- all came rushing out as I stared at my lost friend’s doodle. I knew I would never see Sam alive again and that reality made me incredibly sad. I couldn’t even finish the cross. I left the wood and the tools up in the tree house and headed inside. At that moment, I needed to hug my Mom.

Chapter 16

"Mom...." came Mark's quiet voice, "did Sam ever come home?"

"Oh Marky. No. No, Sam never came home. By this point we all knew she was gone."

"Well, everyone did everything they could, right Mom? To find Sam?" asked Ryan, coming up behind me to squeeze my legs.

"Did you ever finish that memorial cross, Mom? Mark asked.

"Yes, we finished it. In fact, I can't believe it, but, yes, yes...I actually think I still see it there. Let's go see."

I had not set foot on this corner lot since 1989, the same year that I graduated high school. I walked hand-in-hand with my two boys, heading toward the trees, wading our way through the muck of weeds and garbage.

"Be careful guys, watch where you step!" I warned, seeing broken bottles and glass in our path.

As we approached the trees, the wind picked up, just enough to make the leaves rustle. I could hear laughter

– our laughter – echoing. This place had a memory. It knew things. It *remembered* things.

"Mommy," Ry began, "which tree was Sam's favorite?"

We walked to the last tree and standing there, still, was the cross we made. Bending down, I pulled some of the longer weeds that masked the cross. Thick, spikey weeds had grown and wrapped themselves around the cross, almost holding it in place – *keeping it in place*, here, all these years. Honestly, I was surprised it was still there. Nearly 30 years had passed since we placed it there and no one had moved it or broken it. It had been 28 years since we moved from this block, and countless new owners had moved in. Surely other kids may have played down here – or at least had drinking parties on our trees, judging by the plethora of beer bottles.

Yet, there was her cross. Damaged, broken, decaying, faded – but still here. I sat down on the grass and started to cry. My boys sat down too, quietly, neither saying a thing. Just resting their little hands on my knees. One on each side of me.

Looking up I remembered making this cross as well as the moment we placed it here for Samantha. In its glory day it was multi-colored like a rainbow – that was

Mia's idea. The top had a sun painted with a smiley face. The middle – along the horizontal cross arm – said *Samantha Ferris*. Then, vertically down the other cross arm, was written – *our best friend*. The back of the cross had a horse head, Matt drew that, and little hearts and flowers, I drew those. All very colorful when we first did it.

Now, today, you could read most of Samantha's name, although the end had cracked off so the "l" and "s" were missing. The sun was still visible, but the rest was mostly blackened with age. However, it was *still here*. I believed, in that moment, that it was still there for a divine purpose. Being able to show my children, as well as to tell them the entire story of my friend and all the mistakes we made – *I made* – and how even after all of these horrible things happened we still did not learn a lesson. Well, that was definitely a divine purpose.

My mind went so clearly back to when this cross was made, I could see each of my friends' faces as we crafted this piece for our friend.

"Kayla , do you have the red?" squeaked Mia as she continued to paint the rainbow on the cross.

"Yeah, here ya go," I threw her the bottle of paint.

We had been working on the cross in my backyard all day. It was nearly done. We had all taken turns coloring or drawing on her cross. Jessi had the best handwriting, so she wrote Samantha's name on the cross before we started to color the rest in. Even Kyle drew a little frown face toward the bottom of the cross.

"When are we going to put it down there," asked Matt.

"I was thinking guys, we should have like a memorial service. You know, light candles, bring flowers, bury the cross in the ground, say a few words," I suggested.

"Yeah, definitely. Maybe we can do it after dark, you know, so the candles show up," suggested Jessi.

"I dunno," Matt interjected, "my Mom has been really funny about me being anywhere after dark."

"If we all go together, you know, in a group, nothing can happen to us, right?" Jessi asked.

You would think that in the wake of everything that had happened we would all be a little more sensical than this. That we would, out of fear alone, not be willing to sneak out and go anywhere after dark. Well, as I said in the beginning, we were badly behaved children. More than that, we were *children*, ergo we did not always think before we acted. Plus, we were acting out of sadness for our friend. When all was said and done, we agreed to sneak out ....*don't even say it*...and meet down at Starbort and Port at 9:00 pm. In an effort to be safe, we were going to go in pairs. Jessi would come to my window, we would go to Matt's window together then go to Mia's. We agreed to be back home no later than 10:00.

This was a bad idea. That little voice is talking to me again. . .

That night at 8:55 pm I heard Jessi tapping at my window. I closed my bedroom door and locked it, then I opened the window and slid out effortlessly. We hurried down to Matt's and found him sitting on his side step.

"Dude, why you out already?"

"My Mom went to bed early and my Dad is working the night shift."

We all ran across to Mia's and tapped on her window. The curtains moved and she held up two fingers – meaning two minutes. We went to the back and waited. She came out, gently closing the door behind her. We grabbed the cross from behind her garage and headed down to the corner.

"Got the candles and matches," Jessi announced.

"Cool. I have a little shovel to dig the hole and grabbed some rocks to put around the bottom," I answered.

We walked silently through the now-growing grass, as not to alert Mrs. Maloney to our presence, and stopped by the last tree.

The sadness was absolutely palpable.

I bent down and started digging a small hole for the cross. When I was done, we all placed it in the hole. Then we all placed one rock around the base. Standing up, we lit the candles and stood, silently, looking at the cross. Each of us having our own memories of Sam, and each of us grieving differently.

"Um…I just want to say that Sam was such a good friend to me," Jessi started, "she always shared her new toys, made sure I got the green Freeze-E pop 'cause it was my favorite, taught me how to curl my tail with her curling iron. She was fun to be around and it really fucking sucks that she is not here any more….."

Matt began, "Sam was uber cool. She could do a flip off my pool stairs better than any one of us. She was also wicked fast in a race. For someone so small, it was hard to beat her when she got to running!"

125

"Remember when we had that race from the corner to Jessi's house and Sam beat us all by like, literally, 5 minutes!" Mia recalled, "Not only was she fast, but she was smart! Remember how she would hide when we played Ghosts In The Graveyard? Always UP high instead of low so we would walk right under her? Or, how she hid in the spiderwebs at Mr. Jonas' house and we all couldn't find her? Then she jumped out and yelled 'BOOOOOO' and Matt almost peed his pants?"

"I DID NOT!" Matt retorted.

"I remember that Sam would always do anything we asked her and never, ever complained about it. She would give you whatever color in the crayon box you wanted. She would give up her spot on the bed during sleepovers. She would never argue when we picked a cartoon she didn't want to watch, even though she hated Scooby Doo! Sam was the gentlest person I have ever known and it sucks ass that this happened to her! I should have been ME. NOT SAM! ME!!" I yelled.

Turning away from the group, my eyes burning with tears. I dropped my candle on the ground and started swearing under my breath!

"You had better pick up that candle before you burn down all these trees, Kayla," I heard a familiar voice say.

Looking up I saw my Mom. In fact, I saw all of our parents carrying flashlights and looking none-to-pleased.

Chapter 17

"What were you thinking? Have you learned nothing at all from this?" my father demanded angrily!

The cacophonous questions being thrown at all of us in unison created a rather unsettling murmur of concern, anger, fear and disappointment. Before any of us could answer the questions or respond to the accusations, Pastor Rider stepped through the crowd. He looked at the cross we had placed there, and turned to address the crowd:

"Parents, friends, neighbors. I know that you were all afraid. Are still afraid. I know that what you have all gone through is not something that you ever forget or that the fear ever goes away. I also know that each of you wants to tighten your grip on your children, to keep them safe, to protect them from all the evils of the world. I understand and I sympathize. These children are scared, too. These children are grieving their friend. These children are trying to come to grips with the fact that the world is not a safe place. No one should ever have to go through this. No parent should ever lose a child. No child should ever lose a friend like this. Look at the beautiful memorial cross they have made for Samantha. They are processing this loss in a natural and healthy way. They are honoring their friend. I

plead with you, do not be angry with your children. Embrace them. Comfort them. Be understanding with them. Grieve WITH them. Support them. Love them. Help them to feel safe in your arms."

Suddenly, there was whispering from the crowd. As I looked up I saw Stephanie, her Mom and her Dad walking through the crowd of people. They walked right up to where we stood and Stephanie looked at the cross, then to me, then back to the cross. Tears started to fall down her cheeks. She practically jumped forward to hug me. Holding me so tight I could barely breath. Sobbing, quietly, in my ear and whispering, "Thank you, Kayla...thank you....thank you..." and then she released me and moved on to Mia, then Matt, then Jessi. Uttering the same words to all of us. Her Mom was crying and her Dad had his hand around her waist. He had not left her side since Sam had gone missing. It made me feel bad that I had thought such bad things about him.

"Did you kids do this for Sam," asked Mrs. Ferris?

"Yes, Mrs. Ferris, we thought it should go right here, by her favorite tree," Jessi responded.

"We used all her favorite colors," chimed Mia.

"And we made sure to put it deep so it wouldn't fall over," Matt volunteered.

We all looked up at the Ferris' – minus one. We knew that of all of us, their grief was insurmountable. That nothing would ever make them feel whole ever again. But, we also knew how much this memorial meant to them, Stephanie especially. For that, we felt a moment of peace.

Chapter 18

The atmosphere on our block had irreparably changed. It was as if no one could get out from under the gloomy dark cloud of Samantha's disappearance. Eight months turned to a year turned to a year and a half. Life went on, but everything was...tainted. If we found ourselves playing and laughing, we would feel guilty. We did not find the same happiness or joy in the same things, the same activities. We couldn't bring ourselves to actually play at Starbort and Port, but we did visit Sam's memorial often. Sometimes I would go down there alone and talk to Sam. I knew that I wasn't really talking *to* her, but it felt like the only place I could go and have some connection with my friend.

16 months after Sam had gone missing Mia's Mom had her third baby, a little boy! She named him Samuel Patrick. When the Ferris' found out that she did this, it was the first time we had seen Mrs. Ferris smile in over a year! She said she was truly touched and felt like maybe a small part of Samantha will live on as long as we all remember her.

Shortly after Samuel was born, Mia came running down to my house, out of breath with red, watery eyes.

"WE ARE MOVING!" she exclaimed.

"What? What do you mean you are moving? Where? When? How far?" I barreled the questions at her.

"Next month. My Dad got a promotion at work and my Mom said that she thinks it is time for a new start, away from the bad memories here. Kayla, I don't want to move! You are my very best friend! I know it is sad here, with Sam gone and all, but I don't want to lose you *too*!"

I felt heartbroken! My best friend in the whole world was moving. It just seemed like everything had changed – was changing – and nothing would ever be the same again. I walked home slowly, thinking of everything that had happened. Walking past the Robertson's house, Mr. Robertson said hello to me. After Samantha's disappearance he had become a much more tolerant man. Even though they were one of the few families on the block without children, they understood our loss. Mrs. Robertson made obscene amounts of baked goods for the search teams, police officers and FBI agents. Pastor Rider jokingly told her, "When Sam comes home we are going to have a bake sale and all your goodies will bring in thousands!" All she did was smile, weakly.

When I walked in the door my Mom turned from the sink to look at me, "Kayla, honey, what's wrong?"

"Mia is MOVING!" I screeched.

"Oh, I know honey. I am so sorry, but it will be a great new start for Mia in a great, new school district and they will have....."

"I DON'T CARE!" I yelled, "I don't care if she gets a big, new house and a new school and it is a great place with lots of new friends. It is not *here*! It is not with *me*! I can't believe you knew she was moving and did not tell me! I hate this!"

Storming off to my room, slamming my door behind me, the tears started to fall before I could even plop down on my bed. *Why does everything happen to me? Do I deserve to have all these horrible things happen to me? Who am I going to tell my secrets to? Who am I going to talk about boys with? Who is going to have sleepovers with me?* In the midst of my pity-party for one, my Mom snuck in and sat on my bed, "Kayla, honey, it will be OK. I promise. There are going to be a lot of changes in the next few years. In fact, there was something we wanted to tell you tonight at dinner, but I think I would like to tell you now."

"What is it, Mom?" I asked, turning to look at her.

"Well, your father and I were thinking that maybe it would be a good idea since Mia's family is moving and your Aunt and Uncle are moving and....."

"WHAT? Is everyone moving?" *Jesus Christ! Was anything going to stay the same?*

"Kayla, you may not understand this now, but you will someday. Sometimes, when things happen like what happened to Sam.....well, people can't get over it. They cannot resume normal life without the horrid memories tainting everything. It is too hard to live across the street from the Ferris', to see them coming and going and knowing that Sam is not with them. It is too hard for all of us to think about raising our kids here when it feels *unsafe*. Your father and I agree – and Mia's parents and your Aunt and Uncle too – that it is time to bring some new memories, some happiness and some security into your life. Do you understand?"

I did not understand. I felt betrayed. I felt like a giant conspiracy had been perpetrated against me, against all of us. Did none of them understand that we just wanted things to go back to normal? Just to continue on with our lives and try to remember Sam in a good way. How would moving away help us to do that? How would I talk to my friend if I could not visit her memorial anymore? How could I make another best friend? Best *friends!*

I buried my head in my pillow and my Mom stayed there, rubbing my back and letting me cry. She stayed there for a long, long time. Eventually, I fell asleep. When I awoke it was dark outside. I wandered into the kitchen to find my Mom and Dad having a conversation over coffee. I sat down.

"Kayla, honey, are you OK?" my Dad inquired.

"Yeah. I am just peachy keen," I responded, snippily.

"Give her some time, honey, she will be OK," my Mom soothed him.

No. I would NOT be fine! I was not going to ever, ever be fine again! This whole thing sucked! Everything sucked. Samantha being taken sucked. Losing my friends sucked. Moving to a new placed sucked. My life at that moment sucked and no one seemed to give a damn!

Chapter 19

"So, did you move then Mom?" Mark asked. "I mean, Grandma and Grandpa don't live here, so I assume."

"Yes, and it was much faster than I expected, but my parents wanted to get me moved before the school year started up again. The plan was to start high school in our new town. So, they put the house on the market and it sold really quickly, considering. I never thought anyone would buy a house next to a church, but it sold. I found out later it was because the price was so low. Unfortunately, because so many of our neighbors were selling and what had happened on our block the real estate lady told my parents to reduce the price to entice buyers."

"What does 'entice' mean?" asked Ryan.

"It means to make some want something," Mark told his brother.

Huh. I guess all his brain cells weren't quite dead yet.

"So, is that when you guys moved to Michigan?" Mark asked.

"Yes. We moved to the house where Grandma lives now," I informed him. "It really was a very nice house.

I had a huge room with a bay window, a walk-in closet, and a secret hideaway room in the attic. Grandma's sewing room was my room."

"Did you move after Mia, Mom, or before?" Ry asked.

"Ironically, their house did not sell as fast as ours did. Mia's Dad had gone on and rented an apartment near his new job and Mia, her Mom, sister and baby brother stayed behind for a while to sell the house. When our house sold it was a very sad time for Mia and I."

I remembered the month before we were moving to our new city. 30 days seemed like a long, long time but went by in the blink of an eye. Jessi's parents were not moving, nor were the Ferris'. Stephanie told us during one of her rare occasions out of the house that her Mom couldn't "leave her sister behind." I suppose when you have no proof that your daughter is actually dead – like, no body – that the idea of moving away seemed odd. One good thing that happened is that Mr. Ferris left his girlfriend, aka "the alibi," and came home to live with his ex-wife again. She really needed the support, and so did Stephanie.

The Delaneys moved out like they had moved in: under the cover of darkness. The "For Sale" sign went up after they had already moved away. It was all very 'hush hush' and no one knew where they went or what happened to Star. Matt, of course, concocted a story that the local vampire hunters had found them and they felt they had to move before they all got staked in their sleep. The Smiths stuck around for a long time. Apparently, Mrs. Smith got pregnant again and had the baby. Jessi reported to me that she would walk the baby down to the corner and just stare at the lot, then walk back. Mr. Bartlett and Mr. Jonas moved a week before Mia finally moved. Mr. Jonas told her that they had gotten a loft in the city. He felt lucky because it had a rooftop garden that he could fix up with plants and flowers. He also told her that the sadness of what happened made it impossible for him to stay, as he thought of all of us like his adopted kids. He was a very kind man. I heard years later when I was interviewing for a legal job in the city that Mr. Bartlett had died of some odd disease that made him get lots of sores all over his body. I guess it was called AIDS. That made me sad, too, even as an adult.

Mrs. Maloney stayed on the block for about a year after we had all moved. One day she fell down her front steps and broke her hip. Jessi said that her daughter came to take her to live with her while she recovered, but she never came back. Mrs. Maloney never got over what happened to Sam. I remember her telling my Mom that it was "her fault" and that "if she had just been home, maybe Sam would be OK." I guess we all had a bit of guilt about Sam.

The day that I was leaving I was saying goodbye to my friends and went to say goodbye to Mrs. Maloney. She was sitting on her porch, rocking in her chair.

"I came to say goodbye Mrs. Maloney. We are leaving to go to the new house now. I am not sure I will be back. I just wanted to say thank you, you know, for letting us play on your trees and stuff. I was wondering if you could keep an eye on Sam's cross for me?" I asked.

"Sure Kayla, no problem at all. I will make sure the lawn people keep the grass short so it can be seen. Listen, I want you to have this," she said as she reached into her pocket. "This, is a cameo, do you know what a cameo is?"

"No, I don't."

"A cameo is a brooch, like a pin. You wear it on your clothes like a decoration. My Henry gave me this brooch when we got married. It is very special to me. It is a pure pearl base with an ivory engraved silhouette on the front. When I look at the silhouette now I see something different, can you tell what I see?" she asked.

I took the brooch gently from her hand. I look at the pretty pink shell-like background and then at the silhouette on the front. It looked like Sam! The hair, the little nose, the mouth. It really did look like Sam! "This looks like Sam!" I exclaimed, excitedly,

"Yes, I thought so too. Would you keep this for me? Keep it close to your heart. I never forgot my Henry because I had this brooch. Now I think it is time for you to have it."

I jumped up and hugged her tight. "I will always keep it close to my heart. Thank you!"

Reaching into my purse, I pulled out the brooch. I handed it to Mark.

"Is this it?"

"Yes, this is it. I have kept it all these years in my jewelry box. I have worn it only two times since Mrs. Maloney gave it to me. The second time was when I married your father. I hid it on the back of my wedding bouquet. I felt like Sam was there with me that day."

"When was the first time you wore it Mom?" Ryan asked. "You said you have only worn it twice."

Chapter 20

Life in my new neighborhood ended up being quite fine, better than I expected when I left my old house kicking, screaming, pouting and stomping my feet. No. Really. I, at 14 years old, kicked and screamed, cried and threw a major fit because I had to move. Full-on, 100 percent drama-queen-irrific. However, within a few weeks of moving to my new house, I had made friends, gotten the lay of the land, and felt overall better about where we had moved. Mia came to visit me a few times at first, but once her family moved we were too far apart for the casual visits. For a while we kept in touch via phone and letters, but once Mia got a boyfriend and I started high school there was less and less communication with my old friend. I never forgot her, though. We were very important to each other and tried to carry that into adulthood. However, we went to different colleges, made different choices in life, and overall grew apart. We did support each other through some very important and sad times in our life. Her father died when she was only 21 – heart attack. I was there for the wake and funeral. She stood up in my wedding, and I in hers. I am Godmother to her middle daughter, and we always speak on each other's birthdays and on Christmas. While not ideal, we were always together when it counted – or at least there virtually. Once e-mail and texting came to be it became easier to check in with one another.

The summer after my 17th birthday, three years after we moved from our block and nearly 5 years after Samantha had gone missing, I received a phone call from Jessi. Jessi and I had not really stayed in touch much after I moved, so a phone call from her was a bit of an anomaly.

"Kayla, hi, how are you, this is Jessi," asked my sweet friend.

"Great, actually, how are things with you?"

"Well, not so good. I mean...*I am* fine. Doing well in college, have a boyfriend who I think is the hottest thing ever, I am on the cheerleading squad – *don't even say it*, I know I said I would never, ever..... but I am also on target to graduate with honors. It is not me who, um, listen, there is something I need to tell you."

I already knew before she said one, more word. It was about Sam.

"OK, I am listening," I murmured.

"They found Samantha. Well, her body anyway."

"Oh my God! It has been so long. Are they sure it is her?"

"Yeah, it took a bit for a positive identification which is why I did not call sooner. My mom called me at school and told me she had heard from Mrs. Ferris that they thought they had found her and caught the sick bastard who took her, but they had to make sure it was *her* before they could announce it publicly."

Oh my God, they caught the guy!

"Oh my Gosh, Jess, they actually caught the guy? Who was it? Did they identify him? Where did they find her? I have so many questions."

"Kayla, the police will be calling you soon. Apparently, the man who took her, his name was Frank Henrickson. Kayla, the police are pretty sure that he was the guy with the blue car that you hit with the apple. They will want you to come and identify him in what they call a 'line up.'" That is, if you think you can remember!"

My heart sank.

If that is true, then what happened to Sam, it was really, truly my fault! My apple. My apple hit his car. That crazy, angry man.   I would never, ever forget the crazy eyes on that man. He threatened us. He said we would be sorry. He said he would find out where we lived and we would be sorry! It was me. All me. I did this to my friend. I killed my friend!

I dropped the phone, the room started spinning, and I passed out.

"Kayla! Kayla, wake up!" I heard my Mom talking to me, sounding very concerned.

"I am OK Mom. I am OK. What happened?"

"You passed out honey. I heard you hit the floor. What happened? What were you doing?"

I looked next to me and saw the phone. I remembered. Oh, how I remembered. I picked up the phone and heard the tell-tale buzzing of an off the hook line. I hung up. I looked at my Mom and started crying hysterically. I told her what Jessi had told me. I told her that it was my fault. All my fault. She hugged me and comforted me and told me that it was not my fault. She rocked me for what seemed like hours. Then the phone rang. No good news ever came when that phone rang.

"Kayla, it is Jessi. She is worried about you. Can you talk?"

I picked up the phone, "Hi. Sorry, I kinda freaked out a bit there. I didn't mean to leave you hanging."

"I am glad you are OK. I knew you would have a bad reaction. I had a bad reaction too. I felt, um, guilty. Like the stupid game caused all of this."

So, she understood, too. Even though she never actually played.

"Kayla, there is more I need to tell you. Perhaps you should sit down. Samantha was murdered by him Kayla, but not right away. He kept her for a few years and, um, did *things* to her. Brutal things. Sexual things. Mrs. Ferris didn't expand on everything, but I got the gist of it. Apparently, he raped her and kept her chained up in the basement. He beat her and broke some of her bones. This is why it also took a bit longer to identify her, um, remains. When her Mom told the police that her only broken bone was her elbow - you know, from the fall out of the tree - it was harder to identify her because there was more than one broken arm but also her nose, leg, ankle, ribs and the other arm. It threw the police and FBI and investigators who were trying to identify her body."

"Oh my God. I can't.....oh, my God...Poor Samantha....Oh GOD....."

"I know. It is horrible. Apparently, they got a concrete identification by testing her, um, they call it DNA. It is a way to compare her bones, or the stuff in it, to her sister's or parent's and figure out if the bones were related or something. It is a fairly new method and Mrs. Ferris said this was the first time that the local authorities had ever used this technology."

"Where did they find her? How did they find her? "

"Remember how the police said that the car that man was driving was stolen so it was a dead end?"

"Yeah. I remember."

"Well, that man, Frank, he stole that car. Apparently, a few weeks ago he tried to sell the car for real cheap by putting a listing for it in the paper. When the man who bought it from him went to transfer the title to his name, Hendrickson did not have the title or any of the paperwork that goes with a car, and was real shady about why he didn't have it. So, the new buyer got suspicious and called the police. When the police came to look at the car, the serial number matched the one that was stolen. Then, when they searched the records for the rightful owner, there was a flag or warning on the serial number.

The police went to the address where the man bought the car and found Frank and they took him into custody to question him regarding the car and he pretty much started freaking out and confessing to a bunch of different crimes. The FBI agents were convinced that he had something to do with Sam's disappearance so they carefully questioned him, but he was not confessing to anything regarding Sam. However, they had enough other confessions to warrant a search of his home.

When they went into his basement they noticed a crawlspace and a bad, bad smell. That is where she was, Kayla. Stuffed into the crawl space. Wrapped in plastic bags, with layers of duct tape. Mostly just bones. Barely even buried. And Kayla. He lived only three blocks from us."

"If he lived that close and if the car was reported stolen, how the heck did they not find him when they did all those door-to-door searches?" I asked.

"The police think that when he took Sam he left the area, or the state, to avoid being caught. He has a family cabin somewhere down state apparently. In any case, it was just unfortunate that the car was not at the house when they went to search that block or maybe...maybe...."

"Sam would still be alive," I finished.

Chapter 21

Just as Jessi had predicted, a call came from the FBI. They wanted me to come in, once again reiterate the information about the day I hit the car with that apple, and, hopefully, identify Frank Henrickson as the sick bastard that took and murdered our friend.

I had spent the entire 8-hour ride in silence, peering out the window. As the car wizzed down the interstate the memories of that day became clearer and clearer, almost like watching frames of a movie one by one, coming into focus. My Mom and Dad had gone over the entire event with me once again, assuring me that it was not my fault that this happened. Telling me over and over and over how *lucky* I was. *Yeah, right.* How this man was crazy and he would have taken some little girl at some point. That I can't let this hang over my life forever. While I told them that I understood and would stop feeling guilty, the truth is there has not been one, single day that I have not felt that guilt. I never told anyone about it, never confessed my past sins to my new friends. Occasionally, Mia and I would have a "Sam" moment when on the phone or when we would visit. Something would come up and we would find ourselves saying, "remember how Sam loved to...." and then the sadness would hit us all over again.

Furthermore, once I had children my ultimate goal was to make sure that they never put themselves or their friends in danger making bad decisions. I didn't really want to tell them what happened to my friend because I did not want to scare them about the world or the people in it. Sure, I always gave the cursory *don't talk to strangers* lectures, made sure they were careful about safety in all ways, but I had never told them about Sam. I suppose I felt guilty and ashamed. I pretended to be the all-knowing super Mom who could protect them from anything and everything. I wanted them to feel that safety. I wanted them to believe that there was nothing that Mom or Dad couldn't fix or protect them from. The truth is, that is a lie. We parents try our hardest to protect our children - sometimes too hard - and then the inevitable happens.

Children make bad decisions. Children do not listen. Children think they know it all.

Then, children grow up.

First, they want to go to the next-door neighbor. Then, down the street. Eventually across town. Children want independence and with this independence comes greater risk for bad decision making. We, as parents, need to walk that fine line of giving trust and knowing that they will break it. We need to be aware of what our children are doing without casting a shadow on

who they would become as people. It is, without a
doubt, the hardest thing I have ever done in my life. To
have children, to *know* what could happen to them, and
to let them go anyway.

Parents all have revelations.

Children are children and make bad decisions. It is
just part of the protocol of growing up. Testing
boundaries, rebelling against authority, impressing
peers. It is all part of the childhood agenda. I had
hoped that my children would be perfect angels and
never test the waters of smoking, drinking, drugs or any
other bad substances. I had prayed and prayed that my
boys would think before they acted. *Yeah, that is
realistic*! I was trying to protect them by keeping my
leash so tight that they could barely breath and as a
result Mark was pulling that leash as far as he could go
the other way! Is he a bad kid? No, honestly, he isn't.
However, he was going down a dangerous road, making
bad and, frankly, stupid decisions. He is not thinking
about anything other than the fun of the moment and
that was where this lesson needed to be told. He
needed to see that the decisions we make in life can
and often do, spiral into other events and you never,
quite know where you will end up.

My own shame of my bad decisions as a child were
tainting my parenting of my kids. I would constantly tell

them: *"No! Don't do that! Don't go THERE. Don't play with him!"* However, I never really gave them a reason other than the patented line: *because your father and I say so.* Has that ever really had any weight with any teenage child? I should have told them reasons, made it clear what could happen. What *did* happen. That is my misjudgment and now I was trying to make it right. Just like I tried to make right what happened to my friend Sam.

Chapter 22

When my parents and I arrived in our old hometown things were already changing, albeit slightly. While the neighborhoods were not as dilapidated as they were currently, there were the beginnings of neighborhood change brought on by fear. Houses had bars on the front doors and there were fewer children playing outside than there ever were when we were kids. The shift of atmosphere was already in process, and honestly, had been so before we had even moved. I suppose the rumors of what had happened to Sam would live on for generations and while people would still choose to move into our little neighborhood, surely, they were more protective of their children.

When we pulled into the police station I started to feel a panic attack coming on. I was going to see the man who had hurt – *had killed* - my friend. I was scared. It was explained that he would not be able to see me, but I knew that he would know it was one of us who identified him. What if he got out? What if he found out who it was and came to kill me? My heart started beating, my hands got clammy and I couldn't breathe. My Dad turned around and noticed. He unbuckled his seatbelt, got out of the car, and then slid into the seat next to me. He held me comforted me, whispering "shhhhhh sshhhhh there now..." stroking my hair and telling me how proud he and my Mom were of me.

Proud? How could they be proud of me? None of this would have happened if it weren't for me!

A few minutes later I walked into the police station and was greeted by Officer Montgomery. He was older, of course, but still had the friendly smile. I felt instantly at ease. He took me into a small room where he was going to record my statement.

"Now, Kayla, I know that we have already talked about this incident when it happened, but, it is important that we go over it again. It is important that you are completely honest with me. If anything you said back then wasn't true, now is the time to tell the truth. Do you understand?"

"Yes. I understand. I just want to get this over with!"

"I understand completely. Now, can you tell us what happened before Sam went missing. Tell me about the game you used to play down on the corner of your block."

I took my time and told Officer Montgomery all about the game. Every detail I could remember, which was pretty much everything. I told him about the angry man who chased us up the trees. I told him about the foul language and the threats he made. I told him how I would never, ever forget that man's crazy eyes or face as long as I lived! When I was finished, he thanked me and then told me it was now time for me to participate in the lineup.

"Kayla, this next part may be a little scary, but, I promise you, nothing bad will happen to you. This man has already confessed to so many other crimes that he will be locked up for a long, long time. Plus, he cannot see you, nor hear you. I will be with you, so will your parents and some other officers. OK?"

"What if I can't identify him? What if he is not the man I remember?"

"Kayla, all you have to do is tell us if you see the man who chased you up the tree. He will be older, of course. There will be five other men next to him. If you do not see him, then you say 'I do not see him.' But, if you do, you will tell me which number he is, OK?"

"O-ook," I muttered.

We walked into a room that had a window on the left side. My parents were waiting in there for me, and my Mom grabbed my hand when I walked in.

"Kayla, this is a two-way mirror honey, that means that we can see through it, but the people that will be in that room only see a mirror. Do you understand?"

"Yes, Mom. I get it. I am OK. Let's do this!"

An officer stuck his head out of the door and told them we were ready. I watched as six men entered the room with the two-way mirror, all approximately the same height, skin coloring, hair coloring, clothing styles.

I saw him. He was number 4. He. Was. There!

"Number four!" I yelled, "FOUR! He is number FOUR!"

"Kayla, relax honey. Just hold on and the officer will......"

"Number four!" I yelled again, "I see him, he is number four. Oh my God. He is...."

Officer Montgomery came to my side, placing his hand reassuringly on my shoulder. He held it there a minute before speaking, "Thank you, Kayla. It is obvious that you remember who it was you saw, and you have been very, very brave here."

"I don't feel brave! I feel scared. Petrified!" I announced.

"Kayla, you identified Frank Hendrickson, the man that we already arrested under suspicion of committing numerous crimes, among which is the abduction and murder of Samantha Ferris. With your testimony and with his confession, and all the evidence, there is no way this man will be out of prison in his lifetime. Do you understand?"

I nodded my affirmation.

My parents took me from the police station after my father had a few words with the detectives. Then, we left to go to a hotel so that we could rest before heading back home in the morning. I felt emotionally exhausted, drained, and just plain bad. I hoped beyond anything else that I had somehow helped Samantha find rest and peace. That somehow her soul would be able to go to heaven. That reminded me of something important.

Chapter 23

We found ourselves going back to the old neighborhood a week later. Samantha's parents were finally going to lay their daughter to rest. Everyone was going to be there - my aunt, uncle, Matt, Kyle, Jessi, Johnny, Mia and her parents. It was a reunion of sorts, but a sad one. I had never been to a wake or funeral before so my Mom explained how things would be. My Mom bought me a new dress, in black, and I remembered to wear the brooch that Mrs. Maloney had given me. When my Mom saw it she asked where I had gotten it. When I told her the story she just smiled and said, "Mrs. Maloney was a very smart woman."

There were pictures of Samantha all over the funeral home - and pictures of all of us. When I walked in I saw Mia standing and crying by a collage photo display that had all of us playing, on Halloween, at birthday parties. I went up and hugged her tight.

"Oh Kayla, I can't believe we were all so happy once and now our friend is in that vase up there!" she said, pointing to the front of the chapel.

My mom had explained that it was an urn, but I chose not to correct Mia.

"I know M, it is so sad. I am glad that at least we know what happened and that Stephanie can say goodbye to her sister."

"Have you seen Steph yet," Mia asked.

"I saw her a few weeks ago when I came to, you know, identify him."

"Yeah, my Mom told me about that. Kayla, that was so brave! I don't think I could do it! My Mom told me that the police want all of us to interview and maybe testify in court, and I am so afraid to do it!"

"Mia, I had to do it. You have to do it. We owe her. We owe Samantha that!"

The rest of the wake was a mixture of good and bad memories. Stephanie was pretty much in a haze. Being the twin of a murdered girl is a hard thing to be when thoughts of, "she would have looked just like you" are repeated over and over. At one point I thought Stephanie was going to lose it when she glared at one of her mother's work friends with a stare that said, "you idiot!" I knew she needed to laugh. She needed, more than anything, to just have a moment and not be the twin of the murdered girl.

I hatched a plan to get her outside with all of us so we could cheer her up a little. None of us had really

talked with Stephanie since the abduction and she had
pretty much secluded herself within her house ever
since. When we all moved, Jessi said she never really
saw her outside. Out the back of the funeral home was
a covered deck that had some benches and flowers.
We all met out there and dragged Steph, who did not
want to leave her Mom and Dad alone, outside to sit
with us. I wasn't quite sure what to say so I just started.
"Hey, remember that Halloween when Sam wanted to
be a princess and you told her you would do her make-
up. You were being a witch and had that putrid, dark,
green oily make-up and you put it all over her face?
When she turned to look at herself in the mirror she
freaked out and started to try and wipe it off, but it was
smearing all over her and her dress! When your Mom
came upstairs she thought it was a brilliant costume the
zombie princess?"

"Oh my, I had forgotten about that," Steph said with
a hint of a smile.

"Hey, remember when we were playing ghosts in the
graveyard and Sam tried to hide in the bushes by my
house and a spider crawled down onto her head and
she freaked out and tried to move but her shorts got
caught and she couldn't move, so she struggled and
struggled until her shorts ripped?" Matt remembered.

"I remember when we had a sleepover at my house and we put her hand in water because we heard it would make her pee and it DID," Mia started, "and then she was so mad that she had peed her bed that the next night at home she put your hand in water and you peed the bed, Steph!"

"Oh my, I do remember that! I totally deserved it too! At first, I was so mad, but then we just sat on the floor and laughed and laughed," Stephanie recalled.

We continued on like that for a long time. Telling stories about Sam and all the fun and mischief we had gotten into. Stephanie began telling her own stories, some things that we didn't even know. She told us about that "twin connection" and how they often found themselves thinking the same things at the same time. She was looking happier, laughing and even thanking us for being there for her. It was the happiest and the most "normal" we had felt in years, even with our dear friend's body filling up an urn just inside from where we were.

Chapter 24

The funeral was extremely sad. So many people had come to pay their respects to Sam. Mr. Jonas and Mr. Bartlett came with a huge floral bouquet, Mr. and Mrs. Smith came with their little boy. Mrs. Maloney and her daughter came as well. Pretty much anyone we could remember, including Star Delaney who had turned into a beautiful young woman who looked, dare I say, normal. The church was absolutely packed with people who wanted to say goodbye to Samantha.

The Pastor gave a really good speech - called a eulogy my Mom informed me - about Sam and her short, but full, life on earth. It made me cry when he talked about the benefits of the friendships she had made and how so many of us had shown up to pay our respects. Pastor Rider was there as well, and he gave a shorter speech regarding Samantha and her special "light" and the times that they had spent together. He was clearly distraught and looked years older than he should. I had heard, also, that after we all moved from the neighborhood that his church had sort of lost some of its popularity. I suppose for some attending a church where you are supposed to be thankful for the life that God has given you in a neighborhood where such an inconceivable tragedy has occurred doesn't make much sense and seems nearly oxymoronic.

The burial itself was for family only, but the rest of us went to have lunch at a nearby restaurant. It seemed odd to me to have a party after a funeral, but my Mom told me that it was to celebrate the life of the person who died. I guess that made sense.

At the restaurant there was a sundae bar. I made Sam's favorite - a banana split - with two helpings of cherry and butterscotch. I brought it over to Stephanie with two spoons and asked her to share it with me. She looked at me and smiled. I was glad it did not make her sad.

At the end of the afternoon we all said goodbye to everyone. Mrs. Maloney came up and gave me a tight squeeze and said, "Kayla, I see you are wearing the brooch, that is very appropriate indeed."

"Of course, Mrs. Maloney, I have kept it safe ever since you gave it to me and I will continue to as long as I live, I promise!"

Once I was in the car on my way to the hotel I felt a sort of odd relief. It was if something had finally been settled in a way. My friend was no longer lost. My friend was dead, but I knew where she was. In a way, it sort of gave me peace.

"Hey Mom, before we go home tomorrow can we go to Sam's memorial cross, you know on the corner?"

"Sure honey. We will pick up some flowers on the way over."

Chapter 25

"Mom, did you go back and see the cross thing-a-ma-jig?" Ryan asked.

"Yes, Ry. The cross was in better shape than it is today. Starbort and Port was still relatively maintained, but Mrs. Maloney had only recently moved away. Before I left to go back home, I visited with Stephanie a bit. Mr. and Mrs. Ferris were so grateful for my help in putting Frank Henrickson away. They had a long road ahead of them with a murder trial. When all was said and done they sat through a 3-week trial where this man's lawyers tried to get him off with every dirty trick in the book, including the insanity plea. That didn't work though because he had kept her for many years and had taken care to try and hide her murder. These were not the actions of a crazy man, but just an evil one. The Ferris family had to see evidence and hear testimony that was heartbreaking and disgusting for any family member to have to hear!"

"Mom, did, um, that man go to prison?" Mark inquired.

"Yes Mark, he did. He was convicted of murder in the first degree because it was pre-meditated. When I testified that he had threatened us, the prosecutor could prove that this was not an impulsive act of an insane man, but instead a calculated and well-planned abduction that..."

"Mom, you testified? Like, in court? With a judge and jury and everything?" Mark asked.

"Yes, I did. It was the hardest thing I had ever done. The prosecutor told me that they could use my sworn testimony, but, that if the jury actually saw me and heard me describing it to them that there was a greater chance of conviction. So, after talking it over with Grandma and Grandpa, I decided that it was what I needed to do. In fact, we all testified and identified Frank Hendrickson on the stand, except Stephanie, she couldn't enter the courtroom while he was in there, so she video-taped her identification of him via pictures. However, her testimony really wasn't needed as I had made an identification and they even used my sketch-artist sketch from all those years before."

" So he went to jail then Mom?" Ry asked.

"Oh he went to jail on a life sentence without the possibility of parole. Everyone was satisfied with that judgment and the fact that he would not ever be released in his lifetime."

"Hey Mom, so he is still in jail, huh?" Mark inquired.

"Actually, he died in prison, More specifically, he was killed in prison. Apparently, child molesters are the most hated inmates in prison. About 7 months into his sentence he was beaten to death by 10 or so other inmates. He lived for a few days in the prison hospital, but his injuries were too severe and he ended up dying. I remember Stephanie telling me that when her mom got the call that he was dead that she dropped to her knees and started weeping with relief."

"Mom, you were so brave! To testify and to face that man. That had to be so scary for you!" Mark said.

"Mark, you know what, it was. However, I have been even MORE scared in my life, do you want to know when?"

"I cannot imagine being more afraid of anything than facing the man who had killed one of my friends!"

"I am more scared every, single day that something will happen to you or to your brother! I am afraid of making mistakes as a parent. I am afraid that you will make a bad decision and end up hurt, lost or *worse*. Those fears are deeper than any, other fear I have ever had! That is why we are here. We are here so you can see that bad things *do* happen in this world. That sometimes you take for granted your sheltered little life with your six-foot privacy fence, security system, and secure neighborhood. That when you travel downtown in the middle of the day when you are supposed to be in school, when no one knows where you are, who you are with – *anything can happen!* There are bad people in this world that do bad things. I know this for a fact because I lived through it. Thank GOD I lived through it. Samantha, was not so lucky! I can never, ever go back and rework the past, but I sure as hell can protect the future of my sons!"

"Mom, I, um...I am sorry. I am really, truly sorry. I know I have been doing stupid things. I know I am a pain in the ass. I never really thought anything bad would happen to me, but now I know why you and Dad are so protective of me. I guess I never really thought past the idea I was having at the moment, you know? I guess I just wanted to have fun and be with my friends, and didn't think that I could get hurt or anything. Thank you for telling me about Sam and for letting me know that you were not perfect."

"Perfect? Oh Mark, I was never, and am not now, perfect. I am instrumentally flawed."

"Well, Mom, I kinda always saw you as the 'could do no wrong' mother, you know? I mean, you are a lawyer, you graduated at the top of your class, all my friends think you are so smart. I never imagined you as being disrespectful to Grandma or PaPa. I just sort of assumed that you never caused them any problems."

"Ha ha ha, oh Mark. The next time we go to Grandma's, you ask her about me as a child. I am sure she would love to tell you all about me and my shenanigans."

Hugging both my sons tightly, I knew. I knew that the message had gotten through. I knew that while they would not be perfect, that they would test boundaries, make bad decisions and probably do some really stupid things - that they would at least be more cautious. Perhaps pay more attention to the world around them and have a little dabble of fear and self-doubt that could make the difference between a good and a bad decision.

"Mom, is this why you became a lawyer?" Mark inquired.

"Honestly, yes. Watching those lawyers presenting the case against this man who had killed my friend and knowing that they had worked tirelessly to send him to prison and to get justice for Sam. I admired them. I wanted to help them. As I got older, I wanted to *be* them."

"Mom, is that what you do in court? Do you put bad people in jail?" Ryan asked.

"Well Ry, it was my hope to be a prosecutor but, once I had your brother I found that I couldn't spend all day hearing about these crimes and awful situations with children that could be you or your brother. So, I changed career paths a bit. Now I am a child advocate, but that is a complicated thing to explain right now."

I had spent most of my life contemplating what I could have done differently. How my actions contributed to Sam's death. I had always felt the need to make it right. To make amends for what I had done as a child. Part of me knew it was not my fault, that everyone played their own role. I logically knew that Frank Henrickson was responsible. However, I put a great deal of the responsibility on my own shoulders. It was a giant burden to bear. I had put Samantha into Frank Henrickson's cross-hairs.

When I met my husband and we had discussed having children I was adamant about not having them. When he asked why - repeatedly - I finally told him. He, like everyone else who knew the story, told me it was not my fault. Told me that bad things happen in life, but that if we had children that we would be wiser and more cautious. He assured me, over the many years while I was finishing law school, that children were something we needed, that I needed. He was right. I did want children, but I was afraid. I was afraid that a tragedy would happen to one of mine. Moreso, I felt that I did not deserve them. As ludicrous as it sounds, I felt like I had to pay a debt. I went to law school because I wanted to bring bad people to justice. I wanted to be one of the good guys. I wanted to get vengeance for any injured, raped, murdered or otherwise abused child. I wanted to live my life in retribution.

The problem was, that was not a life.

My husband, love his soul, was infinitely patient with me. Explaining how the guilt and the fear and the shame was not my burden. That I had done and behaved as any other child would have behaved. That I cannot make myself the soul responsible party for the acts of a clearly insane and evil man. He told me that it may have been me or Jessi or Stephanie who was abducted. HIs logical brain was one of the reasons I fell so deeply in love with him.

He was right. We decided to have children.

When Mark was born I was so absolutely thrilled to have a son! I was overjoyed and weepy with joy! However, through the years my old fears and apprehensions about the world crept back in. While I attempted to reign in the crazy, as my husband loves to say, I did end up being overprotective to a suffocating fault. So, now, as my 15-year-old son has shown me exactly how he can rebel against me, I have come full circle and face full on my fears - what if something happens to him?

This is the fear of *every* parent. I realize that now. It is not just my fear because of what I went through in my childhood. We all want our children to be obedient and robot-esque, Stepford children but the reality is - no child will ever be that! Children, by definition, are going to press the boundaries. They are going to fight against authority, succumb to peer pressure, make bad decisions. This is how they learn. This is how we, as parents, teach. We take each situation and we use it to show a lesson and hope, really hope, that they at least hear what we are saying and, eventually, listen to the lesson.

"Mom, I have a question," Mark stated.

"Sure, Mark, ask me anything."

"Well, you said that this man, Frank, was driving down your block, from this direction, right?" he asked, pointing to the main road.

"Yes. He came that way," I said, motioning from the main road and down our block, "and I threw the apple and it hit his car."

"Well, why was he driving down your block?"

"What? What do you mean why was he driving down the block?"

"Did he know anyone here? Your block is sort of closed off from other blocks. You have your street, then the main, busy road there and the field behind here. So, if he was not visiting someone on the block, why was he here?"

In all of these years that thought had never occurred to me. Why was he driving down our block? The police determined that he had no friends or relatives on our block.

"You know Mark, I have never thought about that. I know that during the trial it was discovered that he did not have any friends or relatives on our block. Conceivably, he had no reason to be driving down here."

"Yeah, well, um, that is my point. Maybe he was, you know, looking for someone to take. Maybe, he was just driving around looking for little girls playing alone."

In all this time it had never occurred to me that Frank Hendrickson would have come across Samantha in any other way other than me angering him with the apple. I had never even thought that he was driving down our block looking for children to abduct!

The tears started flowing from my eyes and I was shaking my head fiercely.

Not my fault. Maybe not my fault. Could it really not be my fault?

"Mom, you ok? I didn't mean to make you cry. I was just thinking and...well, you know it didn't make sense and..."Mark stuttered.

Gathering up my son I said, "Oh Mark I am crying because I feel....relief! All these years....all this time I have always blamed myself one hundred percent for what had happened to Samantha. It never occurred to me that Frank Hendrickson was already looking to take one of us. You are such an incredibly smart boy!"

Coming back here was a lesson to teach my children about the evils of the world, the bad things that can happen, the caution that they must take. However, it was also a lesson to me. *It was time to let it go*. It was time to say goodbye to my friend Samantha and to the guilt. It was time to allow myself forgiveness for being a child and making choices like a child.

I bent down next to the memorial cross. All the years of the elements tattering this cross, but yet, it still remained. The years battering it have also battered me. I was never really happy in the moment with my kids because I was always living in the past or, fearing what *could* happen in the future. This meant that I was never living in the now. None of knows when life is going to end. None of us knows when our last conversation with a friend, parent or child will be. We have no way of knowing what twists and turns life will throw at us. All any of us have is now. This moment. This memory. This experience. We all need to cherish each moment that we have with those whom we love.

I silently uttered to Samantha, to God, to myself, *I will always remember you but now it is time to forgive myself. I need to start showing my children the love and light in the world. I need to live in the moment. I need to show them that the world is not so scary when you have family and friends and love. You would want that for me. I want that for me. Goodbye my friend.*

I stood up, looked around my little childhood playground and remembered all the fun and laughter, games and good times that my friends and I had here. I listened and I heard laughing and giggling. I closed my eyes and saw Samantha riding her tree branch horse and yelling, "Giddy up!" It was a good memory and one that I was going to take with me now.

"All right boys! I think it is time we make the trip home, what do ya say?"

As I started walking back to the car each of my boys took one of my hands. I gave each of them a squeeze as we walked along in silence. The wind started blowing again, the leaves rustling on the finger-locking trees. I looked back once more at Sam's cross, almost expecting to see her standing there, waving to me. I turned my eyes forward, into my future, and I knew that this would be the last time that I would ever set foot on this corner.

ABOUT THE AUTHOR

Laura Rissmiller-Dennis lives and teaches in Northwest Indiana. She has two children, both boys, and two furbabies. She has been writing since she was very little, entering, and winning, young author contests when she was just a second grader. She often wrote plays for her neighborhood friends to participate in. The idea for this book has been floating around in her mind for many years and she is thrilled to have it out and onto paper. She is currently writing another book, but who knows how long it will take for this one to come to life.

65164745R10102

Made in the USA
Middletown, DE
23 February 2018